BROKENSTRAW RAIN

CHERI WICKWIRE

Trafford
PUBLISHING™

Order this book online at www.trafford.com/07-1912
or email orders@trafford.com

Most Trafford titles are also available at major online book retailers.

Note for Librarians: A cataloguing record for this book is available from Library
and Archives Canada at www.collectionscanada.ca/amicus/index-e.html

Printed in Victoria, BC, Canada.

ISBN: 978-1-4251-4516-3

*We at Trafford believe that it is the responsibility of us all, as both individuals
and corporations, to make choices that are environmentally and socially sound.
You, in turn, are supporting this responsible conduct each time you purchase a
Trafford book, or make use of our publishing services. To find out how you are
helping, please visit www.trafford.com/responsiblepublishing.html*

*Our mission is to efficiently provide the world's finest, most comprehensive
book publishing service, enabling every author to experience success.
To find out how to publish your book, your way, and have it available
worldwide, visit us online at www.trafford.com/10510*

 www.trafford.com

North America & international
toll-free: 1 888 232 4444 (USA & Canada)
phone: 250 383 6864 ♦ fax: 250 383 6804 ♦ email: info@trafford.com

The United Kingdom & Europe
phone: +44 (0)1865 722 113 ♦ local rate: 0845 230 9601
facsimile: +44 (0)1865 722 868 ♦ email: info.uk@trafford.com

10 9 8 7 6 5 4 3 2

DEDICATION

Dedicated to my children, Shawn, Shane and Erin, and my beloved grandchildren. Thank you for your support and for always being the force behind my dreams and aspirations. May each of you reach to the heavens and bring back a star.

THIS IS the heartwarming story of a couple from Poland who came to the United States at the turn of the century in 1911. Here, Katerzyna Magdalena Kunicka and Jan Pietr Wjotla (Vi-o-la) married and raised a family of seven children on a small farm in northwestern Pennsylvania.

They encountered persecution from the Ku Klux Klan because they were Catholic immigrants. Life in the country was hard and demanding through Prohibition and the Great Depression. Two sons fought in World War II for freedom and democracy.

The youngest son, John Tanner Wjotla, graduated from West Point and served his country valiantly as a secret agent. He and the woman he saved as a small child, kidnapped by the KKK, strive to help each other find the American dream.

Along the Brokenstraw Creek, their story comes alive.

CHAPTER ONE

KATARZYNA ADJUSTED her skirt and straightened her hat before beginning her descent down the gangway. She was anxious to set foot on firm ground. She had spent two weeks rocking and rolling on that old ship. Living amid two hundred women and children in close quarters had been a miserable experience. She would have thrown herself into the sea if the voyage had lasted even one more day.

She had been sick from morning to night. The memory of the storms they encountered made the nausea rise up in her throat. Katarzyna had no idea what adventures were awaiting her in this new country, but she would gladly take her chances on dry ground.

Katarzyna Magdalena Kuzicka had left her village in Poland three weeks before. She left behind her parents and nine brothers and sisters to journey to a new continent. Relatives who had immigrated to America before her had told stories of the streets being paved with gold and great riches to be found. Katarzyna wasn't too sure if she believed all the rumors, but she was more than willing to come and see for herself.

The year was 1911. Many citizens of Eastern Europe's towns and villages believed their children must go elsewhere to find a better future. Katarzyna was the eldest child at fifteen years of age. She was full of pluck and confidence. She could brave the perils of the unknown and find a secure and rewarding future across the sea.

Katarzyna's Uncle Marcie, her mother's brother, had been in the seminary in Poland studying to become a Catholic Priest. He became disenchanted with Poland and had immigrated to America in 1906. He wanted Poland to throw off the yoke of tyranny and be her own country but Poland continued to fall under whatever army chose to take over at any given time. He was sponsoring his sister's oldest child to come to the United States and begin a new life. Marcie had married shortly after arriving in America. He and his wife, Sofia, had two children with another one on the way. His niece, Katarzyna would be a welcome addition to their home. She could help with the children and also assist Sofia, with the household chores.

He had sent Katarzyna a train ticket from New York City to Clarendon, Pennsylvania. They were looking forward to greeting her when she arrived. He had sent her information about Ellis Island. He wanted her to know in advance what she would have to endure while being processed. He had included some cash so she wouldn't have to worry about paying for a taxi or food on the train.

Marcie had cautioned Katarzyna to not travel alone. She was urged to leave with other families from her village, so she would have a male escort once she arrived in America. No single woman would be allowed to set foot in New York City alone. There were too many dangers in the city for a woman traveling without an escort.

Katarzyna glanced back at the ship she had just exited. The gangway was full of immigrants like her, hastily coming down the last remaining part of the ship they had traveled on for such a long time. Children were following their parents, clinging to their hands or pieces of their clothing, all the while looking around in wonder at what was going on. They were curious, even a bit apprehensive, to see what would happen to them in this new and exciting place.

Katarzyna was looking for a friend she had made on the ship. They had promised each other they would not get separated and would go through processing together. It wasn't easy standing there waiting and watching. They were being prodded along like cattle, instructions bellowed out from several voices at once.

The tender which had dropped them off at the dock was now headed back to the massive ship. It resembled a child's bath toy as it bobbed about in the waves in the harbor. The Bremen was the name painted on its side. Katarzyna knew that name would be buried in her memory for the rest of her life. She took a big breath and held it for a long moment. She expelled it slowly and followed the throngs of people as they surged forward. The immigrants were beginning a new chapter of their journey. They entered the doors of the famed Ellis Island. They had arrived. They were finally in this place called the United States of America.

The tags that were pinned on her blouse were fluttering in the ocean breeze. The wind lifted her skirt and blew the ends of her scarf into her face. They had been told onboard the ship to not touch the tags or remove them as they would identify each passenger to the immigration officials. Speaking only Polish, Katarzyna nervously made her way into the building. She wanted to get through the process as quickly as possible.

She kept looking around with hopes of seeing her friend, but found just a sea of unfamiliar faces. Uncle Marcie had told her what to expect, but she found the mass of humanity overwhelming as she was herded into the main receiving area.

The new arrivals were not aware they were being carefully scrutinized as they walked toward the Processing Center. A team of doctors was present as the passengers were discharged from the ship. They were looking for immediate signs of disease and illness. They were Public Health Doctors. They scanned the new arrivals for cholera, tuberculosis, favus (scalp and nail fungus), insanity, and other mental impairments.

Moving three abreast, the immigrants made their way up the stairs to a huge hall, which was the Registry Room.

Katarzyna knew she would have to endure the check by the "buttonhook men". Her uncle had told her it would be painful, but would only last a minute. This was a process by which the doctors checked for trachoma by turning the eyelid inside out, looking for inflammation on the inner eyelid. They used their fingers, a hairpin, or a button-hook to make the examination.

She turned her head when those before her endured the painful examination. She almost broke from the line and ran the other direction but she couldn't move. The mass of people behind her almost crushed her as she was pushed and shoved along. She tried not to think about what was taking place. Finally, it was her turn. She held herself perfectly still as her eyes were examined. The inspector's breath was fetid. She thought she would throw up right in his face. She dared not breathe as he scanned her eyes. In seconds that horrible experience was over and she proceeded into the main hall. A thousand different languages and dialects assailed her as she made her way through the maze of lines separated by metal railings.

The legal inspectors stood behind tall desks, assisted by interpreters fluent in every language. Katarzyna watched and listened as those in front of her made their way to the front of the line and began the interrogation process. The inspectors wore starched collars and heavy serge jackets to offset the incredible chill the room generated with the cold air coming in off the sea.

The inspectors verified the information on the tags. They asked a series of questions already contained on the ship's manifest. Family names were recorded with care, paying special attention to the spelling. Katarzyna was asked her name, occupation, marital status and destination.

In this way they could determine the immigrant's social, economic and moral fitness. The American welfare agencies were already overwhelmed with requests from impoverished immigrants, so those immigrants were expelled from the country that were likely to become "a public charge."

Unescorted women and children were detained until their safety was assured through the arrival of a telegram, letter, or prepaid ticket from a relative.

Fortunately, Katarzyna had a letter and a prepaid ticket in the tapestry bag she carried with her. After displaying these documents, she was allowed to continue down the "Stairs of Separation," so-called because they marked the parting of the ways for many family and friends with different destinations. Katarzyna was directed toward the railroad office and train depot to points west.

The entire process had taken about five hours. Katarzyna was both hungry and very tired. Vendors were selling food and drink near the train depot. She walked over to see what they were offering. She had some paper money her uncle had sent her. She offered the boy the smallest denomination. He gave her what appeared to be meat wrapped in a bread of some sort, and her change.

The food smelled marvelous. Although she had no idea what it was she was eating, she hurriedly downed it. She was hesitant about buying something to drink so she walked over to a drinking fountain to get a drink of water.

Her first food in this new and wonderful country! She pondered for a minute trying to determine what it was she had just eaten. It had smelled so good and tasted so delicious. Surely she could have more in the days ahead!

The depot agent looked at her ticket. With a nod he directed her where to sit and wait for the train to Pennsylvania. Katarzyna looked around to see if she recognized anyone from the ship. She would love to see the familiar face of the young man she had planned to meet when she arrived in America. Jan was a few years older. He had made the trip to the United States on a different ship. They had been together in Hamburg, Germany, but had separated when Jan was assigned a berth on another ship that was leaving the day before The Bremen.

Jan Pietr Wjotla (Vi-o-la) was five years older than Katarzyna. They were from the same village in Poland. They had been planning for many months to leave Poland and begin a new life together in America.

Katarzyna's parents liked Jan, but thought she was too young to give her heart so soon to a young man. The village of Czefkow had nothing to offer young people. Ancestors had farmed the same land for generations. If you weren't the eldest son you were forced to leave and find work elsewhere. Jan had told them he was going to America to make a better life for himself. Katarzyna had talked about nothing else for months, so when Uncle Marcie offered to sponsor her, her parents reluctantly agreed to send her to America, as long as she was under Marcie's care.

Katarzyna and Jan had made a pact that they would travel to Pennsylvania together after they reached America. Jan had promised he would wait for her at the train station. Katarzyna thought it would be an impossible task to find her friend amid this chaotic mass of people. It was only through sheer luck and desperate wishing that Katarzyna spotted Jan standing by one of the signs directing passengers to the train platform. Her heart actually did flip flops at the sight of him. Her stomach turned over as she stared at this friend of hers, someone she knew! She would no longer be alone. Jan stood, holding his hat in his hands. He was constantly twisting it and turning it, all the while searching the area. He was looking for her.

Katarzyna thought he was so handsome. She could only stare at him while she considered how lucky she was he had waited for her to come to the station. Thank God he hadn't left without her.

Being a young woman of good upbringing, Katarzyna was not about to run wildly through the public station and throw her arms around a man. She was about to turn and begin walking directly to him to discreetly say hello when Jan spotted her. He began shouting her name and running toward her.

"Katarzyna, Katarzyna!" he cried, waving his arms. He looked like an excited rooster in the barnyard.

"Excuse me Miss, excuse me Sir," he stammered in broken English. Trying very hard not to knock anyone over in his haste to reach her, Jan collided with a porter pushing a cart with a pile of luggage. They both wound up in a tangled heap on the ground with the enraged porter sitting on his lap!

"Kindly watch where you are going, young man!" the old man bristled as he struggled to stand upright and resume his duties.

Katarzyna began to laugh behind her hands as she covered her mouth in fright watching her friend plow his way through the crowd of people in his haste to reach her. The two of them soon had the attention of everyone in the train station after this raucous scene. It actually helped relieve the tenseness and anxiety everyone felt as they searched for loved ones and the right train that would take them to their destination.

Finally Jan reached her. He began to laugh, both with relief from finding Katarzyna and also in reaction to his bowling over the luggage cart. They laughed and hugged each other until tears ran down both their faces.

They eventually made their way to a bench and sat down to get themselves under control.

"Did you have any trouble getting on your ship in Bremen?" Jan inquired, still breathless.

"No, I traveled to Germany with a couple from Czefkow. They were also traveling to America. I lost track of them when we landed and haven't seen them since. I met a young girl on board the ship. Her name is Bettina and she was a big help to me, but I haven't seen her either. I didn't realize it would be such a busy place when we arrived!"

"There were a lot of men from Poland and Germany on our ship. I came over on the Konig Albert," Jan replied as he adjusted his cap back on his head and spread his long legs out in front of him. "I was traveling with my cousin but he disappeared after we arrived at the immigration counter. He was so anxious to leave Poland and was so excited about settling in Pennsylvania. I hope he catches up with us before the train leaves. This place is just so full of people and boxes and suitcases and everything else under the sun. I am just so frustrated. First I worried about you and now it's Karl!" Jan wiped his face with his hand and his brows came together in a perplexed expression.

"Oh Jan, I am sure he has just been momentarily detained. A lot of people were sent to other areas to be examined or wait for documents."

"I know, but he has come so far. I want him to come with us so he can fulfill his dream of buying some land. He wants to plant a garden of beautiful flowers so he can start his own flower shop."

"I love flowers too," Katarzyna exclaimed while folding her

hands in her lap demurely. "I'm going to have the biggest garden you've ever seen! I want to live on a farm and never have to see the ocean again! Don't you agree, Jan?" Katarzyna looked at him questioningly and saw he was smiling at her. He had a very nice face for a boy, she thought. His eyes were dark, like sunflower buttons and his eyelashes seemed to go on forever. She was certain if she touched them they would be velvet and soft to the touch. His hair was black as coal under his cap. As much as he tried to brush it all under his cap, a lock fell forward in a tousled heap upon his brow.

"I am going to buy a farm! It will have rolling fields and a forest of trees and a creek running through the fields. I never want to see the ocean again either. I thought my insides would burst crossing all that water!"

Jan laughed and leaned back on the bench thinking how lucky he was to have met this nice girl in the old country. Now he wouldn't have to travel alone. He looked at her and smiled. She was so tiny! He loved the way her whole face lit up when she smiled at him. He thought she was very brave to come all this way by herself. He knew his sisters would never have done that. He decided right then and there that he would make sure she arrived at her uncle's safely. He would ask Uncle Marcie if he could court her until he was financially capable of asking for her hand in marriage.

Just as they were ready to board the train, Jan's cousin Karl came running down the platform, his bag half open, his clothes sticking out of the seam, flapping in the breeze, as he raced to board the train. Jan helped his cousin up the steps. As they climbed aboard the train the three of them said goodbye forever to the land they left behind. Katarzyna, Jan and Karl were beginning a new life in America.

CHAPTER TWO

T HE TRAIN ride was slow and the seats were hard and uncomfortable. It was very noisy but the trio didn't care. Just being off the ship was wonderful. Katarzyna was able to sleep most of the way, even though she was very excited about seeing the countryside in this new country. It reminded her of Poland with the green hills and forests.

Jan had brought food along so they talked and laughed and shared a meal before all three of them simply collapsed from sheer exhaustion.

Many people exited the train at various stations along the way. The closer they got to their destination, the more anxious Katarzyna became. By the time the conductor announced Clarendon as the next stop, she was beside herself with anticipation.

Uncle Marcie was there at the train depot in Clarendon to greet her just like he promised. She was so happy to see him. Jan and Karl were met by friends of Karl who were taking them to the farm where they would be working and learning new skills. It was an awkward moment when the time came for her to say goodbye to Jan. She had been looking forward to coming to America and being with him and now they were saying goodbye again.

Jan made the first move by giving her a hug. He told her he would be by to visit the following Sunday. Uncle Marcie wasn't sure of this forwardness with his niece but said that would be fine. He invited Jan to join them for dinner. The invitation made

Katarzyna feel a lot better. She was fairly singing when they left the depot and began the ride into town.

Clarendon was a small town in northwest Pennsylvania. It was surrounded by forests and streams. New factories were springing up and sawmills were an important part of the economy. Dairy farming was also a primary occupation. Katarzyna knew the men worked on the farms and their wives tended to the garden and raised the children. They grew their own food and butchered their own meat. It was similar to Poland except here everyone owned the land or worked the land for a decent wage. Hunting was the main topic of conversation in the fall and winter months. A venison roast for Sunday dinner was welcome in most households. Wild turkeys were abundant and a giant bird graced many a table at holiday time. Uncle Marcie talked about the town all the way home.

Aunt Sofia and the two children were anxiously awaiting the carriage. The children were jumping up and down when the horses pulled into the drive. Aunt Sofia cautioned the children not to get too close to the horses as they ran ahead to greet their cousin who had come all the way from across the sea to live with them.

"Now children, let Katarzyna get down from the carriage before you attempt to greet her" Aunt Sofia remonstrated while laughing lightheartedly at her two children's attempt to climb into the carriage.

"Yes Momma", the little girl said as she stepped back down to the ground and looked sweetly up at Katarzyna.

"My name is Ellie and I am three years old," she remarked happily as she began to dance around the yard.

"And who is this sweet baby boy?" Katarzyna couldn't help but lift the toddler up and hold him in her arms. He was struggling so hard to reach her.

"That's Theodore, our youngest," announced Uncle Marcie as he came around the side of the carriage to help her down.

Katarzyna embraced her new Aunt. She gave the children hugs and kisses before being drawn along into the house. It was a lovely house with gingerbread corners and a wonderful wrap around porch. The entry doors appeared to be at least eight feet tall. Katarzyna didn't miss a thing as she walked into the house. Each door had a panel of beveled lead glass, oval in shape. The entryway was very large. Dark paneling encircled the spacious entry. Rich, thick carpeting covered the floor leading into the main living areas. The children raced on ahead, running up the stairway. They couldn't help but encourage their new houseguest to hurry and see the room they had helped momma fix for her. Sofia led her up the stairs and down the hall. They entered a room which opened off the wide hallway toward the back of the house. It was a beautiful room. The windows overlooked the spacious backyard. Katarzyna could see a lovely rose garden and several maple and elm trees

Katarzyna knew she was going to be very happy. The children were very sweet. She soon became very fond of Aunt Sofia. Every Sunday Jan would come to town. They would sit together in church. Afterward they would walk to Uncle Marcie's for dinner. In the afternoon the house would fill with other family members. The men would always ask Jan to join them in playing pinochle. They would laugh and slap him on the back when he declined. They knew all along he just wanted to spend time with Katarzyna. Soon he would be one of them. The men figured it was just a matter of time before Jan and Katarzyna would wed, then the children would begin coming. Soon she would be spending the afternoons with the womenfolk and Jan could drink beer and play cards with the men.

A few months later Jan moved into town and took a job at one of the new factories. He wanted to make more money and be closer to Katarzyna. He often joined his cousin on weekends working on the farm to earn extra money. He was saving everything he could so he could buy some land and finally be able to ask her to marry him.

The first year passed very quickly. Katarzyna now had three children to care for. She was happy and content. Uncle Marcie and Aunt Sofia were very good to her and she was learning to speak English. Aunt Sofia was teaching her to cook and clean. She quickly became adept at canning vegetables and baking bread. Her sewing skills improved and she learned to knit and crochet. Soon it became evident that she was ready to settle down and create a life for herself and Jan.

Jan made a beautiful chest for Katarzyna to celebrate their second Christmas in America. She loved the chest. She couldn't wait to fill it with everything she would need when they married. She spent every spare moment sewing pillow cases and embroidering them with flowers. She made tablecloths and crocheted doilies. Aunt Sofia helped her make her wedding dress of white satin. Together they tediously sewed pearls on the bodice. It was so beautiful.

The couple was popular with everyone in town. They were always invited to all the social gatherings.

This one day, Jan and Katarzyna were on their way to a wiener roast at the home of a friend just outside of town. It was a beautiful fall day. The air was crisp and just right for a bonfire. The leaves on the trees were gorgeous in their red and gold splendor. The dry leaves that had fallen crunched under their feet as they walked along the dirt road leading to the farm.

They were holding hands and swinging their arms as they continued down the road. Suddenly, Jan stopped and drew her into a grove of trees just off the road. He grabbed her to him and kissed her hard on the mouth. She responded in turn and they were both breathless as they came apart. Katarzyna started to say something but Jan softly placed his hand over her mouth as he began to speak.

"It has been over two years since we came to America, Katarzyna. I think we should get married in the spring. I've found some land in Warren County and it has a house on it. We would have to build a barn and get some livestock, but I think we could make it work. Will you marry me, my love?"

Jan had said everything quite fast and Katarzyna was trying to catch up on all he had said, but she definitely heard the very last sentence clearly!

"Oh yes, Jan, yes, I will marry you! Right now, in the spring or the summer or whenever! I love you Jan!"

The couple threw their arms around each other and began dancing around the trees until they fell to the ground laughing and trying to catch their breath. Jan looked into her eyes and held her face in his hands as he lowered his lips to hers and they kissed until they were breathless again.

"We really must get up and go on to the hayride," Jan said. "We'll have plenty of time for all this kissing once we're married! He offered her his hand and pulled her to her feet. Get up my beautiful bride-to-be. Let's go tell our friends the good news!"

Katarzyna jumped to her feet and danced ahead of him down the road. Suddenly she stopped and ran back to him and kissed him full on the mouth! Her face flushed she dropped her eyes and then looked at him again. His eyes reflected his love for her as he grinned from ear to ear.

She grabbed his hand and together they continued down the path, talking excitedly about the land and what they would grow and how many children they would have.

Before they got to the gate and turned into the lane leading to their friend's house, Jan once again stopped and turned to Katarzyna.

"What is it, Jan?" Katarzyna asked, worried when she saw the serious look on Jan's face.

"There's one more thing I think we should discuss before we see our friends," Jan replied as he gazed off into the distance. A moment passed and then he turned to her and said, "I think we should change our names. You will be Katie and I will still be Jan but I will spell it like the Americans do, J o h n. What do you think?"

Katarzyna walked over to a stand of maple trees and slowly walked around it playing her fingers along the bark. Looking all around her she paused in serious thought. Jan was beginning to think he had suggested something very wrong. He was about to walk over and apologize when she suddenly stopped and strode back toward him in a very determined fashion.

"I think it is an excellent idea!" she shouted, loud enough to send the birds flying in fright from the limbs where they had been roosting. But, we will keep your last name, won't we?"

"Of course, my darling Katarzyna! Excuse me…. Katie! Now remember, from now on it is John and Katie."

"This is so exciting! I can hardly wait to tell everyone!" Katie exclaimed.

"It is settled then, Katie. You set the wedding date and I'll begin working on the house. My friend Walter said he would help. We'll get some chickens and Walter said he would give us a couple cows to start off with. I'll work at a factory during the day and work the farm too. We'll have a good life Katar…I mean Katie."

Laughing they ran the rest of the way to greet their friends and tell them the news.

Katie was so excited she hardly remembered the day at all. They had a great time with their friends but her mind was awhirl thinking of ideas for her wedding and knowing she was about to become a wife and then soon a mother with babes of her own! Oh, it was just too much to think about!

John was thinking he had just made the biggest decision of his life. He knew in his heart that he had made the right decision in coming to America. He loved Katie with his whole being and he just knew they would make it. He would always remember this very moment and how happy he felt. Whatever life held for them he was sure they could deal with it as long as they were together.

CHAPTER THREE

THE MONTHS seemed to fly by. Uncle Marcie gladly gave the couple permission to marry. Both he and Sofia loved the young couple dearly. They had watched the romance blossom and knew the day would come when the two would leave and make their own way into the world.

John and Katie, as they were now called, had taken all the right steps in planning their wedding. Months of making furniture for their house had consumed most of John's spare time. He wanted everything to be perfect when they arrived at their farm.

Katie had worn everyone in the family out constantly chatting about the wedding. First she was happy and dancing around and then she would get woeful and sad because her family couldn't be there. The next second she would be picking Ellie up and twirling her around, much to the little girl's delight. "You'll be so beautiful as my flower girl, Ellie."

"Will I be a princess Katie?" asked Ellie, tilting her head and looking up at her cousin.

"Even prettier, my sweet!" replied Katie. "You'll be the prettiest one in the church!"

"The bride is always the prettiest one, silly" laughed Ellie. "You will be the prettiest and John will be the most handsomest!"

Katie loved every bridal shower she went to. Her friends gave her many wonderful gifts. She was sure she would never use all of the beautiful linens she received. She would miss all the friends she and John had made since they came to Clarendon. John promised her some day they would come back and see everyone.

The wedding day dawned sunny and warm. It was a perfect day for John and Katie to be married. Families and friends had looked forward to this weekend event for months. Aunts and uncles, nieces and nephews, cousins and friends had been arriving in Clarendon for days. Many hours had been spent in the kitchen cooking and baking. Vats of sauerkraut had been brought up from the cellar and the odiferous odor of cooked cabbage with kielbasa permeated the house day and night. Dough for pierogies and pastries and breads gave the kitchen delicious yeasty smells. Pits were dug behind the house to cook the meats. Pork, beef, various kinds of sausages and dozens of chickens were being prepared for the marriage feast.

The wedding was scheduled to take place at eleven o'clock on Saturday morning. The little Catholic Church would be filled to overflowing. Following the wedding everyone would return to Uncle Marcie's home for the beginning of the festivities. Dinner would be served and then the bride and groom would retire for a nap while their guests partied or took naps too. Upon awakening, the couple would open their wedding gifts and everyone would admire them. Following another meal everyone would party into the night. On Sunday there would be another mass to bless the marriage and following that would be another meal. Immediately after the dinner, the couple would finally descend with their belongings and once the wagon was loaded they would depart for their new home which was about thirty miles away.

Katie was sitting on her bed staring into space the morning of the wedding. She was in silent thought when Aunt Sofia knocked and entered her room.

"Are you ready for today, Katie?" her aunt inquired while throwing back the curtains and welcoming the sunshine. She walked over to the bed and put her hand on Katie's shoulder, bending down to peer into her face. "This is the most important day of your life sweetie. I hope you are sitting here thinking of John and not feeling sad."

Katie turned to her aunt and absentmindedly began drawing patterns on the bedspread. "Aunt Sofia, I love John. I can't wait to marry him. I'm just feeling a little sad because Mama and Papa aren't here to see me get married. I miss them and my brothers and sisters so much."

"There, there my sweet child," the older woman murmured, patting the young woman's hands. Getting down on her knees so she could look into the face of her young charge, Sofia lifted Katie's chin and said ever so gently, "don't waste tears over what cannot be changed Katie dear. Your Mama and Papa are always here with you in your heart. Be the woman they would want you to be and always strive to make them proud that they sent you to America. They are thrilled you are going to become the bride of Jan Wjotla."

Katie hugged her aunt. She jumped to her feet and asked her to help her get dressed. The beautiful wedding dress was perfect on Katie. She loved the feel of the satin as it slid down the length of her body. It was a special moment when Sofia placed the Polish wedding veil on her head. It was the last gift she had received from her mother, given to her on the day she had left for America. Soon the two women were chattering like sisters and giggling like schoolgirls. They were soon joined by several more women and girls who were fussing over Katie and exclaiming what a beautiful bride she was.

The walk to the church was an event in itself with children running along side the bridal party, tossing flowers and chanting good wishes along the way.

Upon arriving at the church everyone went inside until only Katie and Uncle Marcie were left standing outside the entrance. He was smiling down at her. He asked if she was ready to begin the walk down the aisle to her beloved John.

As she nodded yes, the doors opened and the music from the old organ began filling the ancient church. All eyes were on the bride as she began her walk down the aisle toward the groom.

John stood so straight and tall. He was so handsome in his new suit. Katie couldn't take her eyes off him and he couldn't take his eyes off her.

"She is so beautiful" John whispered to no one in particular. Katie was sure she was living a dream. When the priest uttered the words, "Do you Katarzyna Magdalena Kuzicka take this man Jan Pietr Wjotla to be your wedded husband, to have and to hold from this day forward....?" She answered as if in a trance, all the while staring into John's eyes. Each was lost in a world of their own.

The people who witnessed the wedding all agreed it was one of the most beautiful weddings they had ever attended.

Katie and John signed their names on the marriage certificate for the last time as Katarzyna and Jan. This new day and new chapter in their lives would begin as Katie and John Wjotla.

The afternoon was so much fun. Katie and John danced on the lawn until she thought she would fall over in exhaustion. The money dance seemed to go on forever. The couple received lots of money to help them settle down as newlyweds.

Katie was delighted when one of her closest friends caught the bridal bouquet. Everyone teased her boyfriend who was merrily getting drunk, helped in this endeavor by all the men hanging out by the beer kegs.

Finally it was time to retire to her room and change her clothes. She was excited about leaving Clarendon and finally seeing her new home. She had to give herself a pinch to make sure she wasn't dreaming. She was a married woman!

John was taking all the ribbing from the men in good spirit. He was anxious to be on their way. He soon changed into working clothes and soon he and the other men had the wagon ready to go.

CHAPTER FOUR

THE FIRST days of Katie's marriage to John were even happier than she had anticipated. John was considerate and warm and very loving. They were having a great time riding through the countryside. They were both very anxious to get to their new home and begin their lives as a married couple.

Katie rejoiced on their wedding night after realizing the passion she brought to their marriage bed was equal to that of her husband. They loved without caution or worry, abandoning all sanity to the wind. They considered their honeymoon to be the greatest ever experienced by two people. By the time the wagon entered their very own country lane they were certain no one had ever loved each other more than they.

Their new house sat at the bottom of a small hill with a broad expanse of lawn in the front. It was a beautiful little white cottage. It had a fruit cellar underneath the house and an attic over the main floor. The house had a small porch in the front. The back door led into a mud room. There were hooks on the wall to hang their coats. Behind the house was a stone pathway which led to the outhouse. A little ways beyond that stood a small chicken coop.

Katie loved the house at first sight. She walked through the house marveling how nicely John and Walter had remodeled the interior. She didn't know what to expect after John first described the old house. New flooring was added to the kitchen and the hardwood floors throughout the house gleamed with new stain. The attic had been divided into three large bedrooms although they remained unfinished. They would use the large bedroom downstairs. John had covered the walls with lavender flowered wallpaper for her as a wedding present.

A neighbor had given John a cooking stove. They had brought dishes, pots and pans, quilts and even a rocking chair they had received as wedding gifts. John had made their bed out of cherry wood. He had also constructed a table and four chairs. Uncle Marcia and Aunt Sofia had given them a sofa for a wedding present. They would have to purchase an icebox. John promised to build more cupboards in the kitchen.

John made up the bed while Katie began unloading her chest full of linens and curtains she had made. The tablecloth her Baba had given her in Poland was tucked away in a bureau drawer for special occasions. There were a few old rugs in the house and these she brought out into the yard and beat them until dust flew in every direction. She danced around the yard laughing and waving her hands in the breeze until she fell over in the grass. She just laid there looking at the sky and that's where John found her, fast asleep, all tuckered out from a busy day in their new home.

The next day dawned warm and sunny. Katie decided the first order of business was to plant the weeping willow tree cousin Karl had given them for a wedding gift. He said it reminded him of Katie when he saw her dancing. He said when the branches swayed in the wind it would be like watching Katie dance on her wedding day.

In the weeks that followed, John and his friend Walter finished the cupboards in the kitchen and began to formulate plans for the barn. It was important that it be up before winter came so the hay could be put in and the cows and horses would have shelter from the cold and snow. This part of the country received a lot of snow in the winter. There was plenty of timber on the property to use to build the barn.

One fine Saturday the yard was filled with lumber and pulleys and tools as neighbors from all around gathered to put up the Wjotla barn. Katie had cooked for a week, but she didn't have to work so hard because all the neighbor ladies showed up carrying dishes of food, breads, jelly and wonderful desserts. The women took care of the food while the men built the barn. Everyone left in the evening to take care of their livestock, but early the next morning they all returned to finish the job. John and Katie were very thankful for having such good people as their neighbors and friends. It was a wonderful feeling to know you could count on each other when help was needed.

John was working full time at the tannery in nearby Spring Creek. He arose early to take care of the livestock and milk the cows. He rode one of the horses to work in the summer. In the winter he often caught a ride into town with a neighbor down the road who also worked at the tannery. When the weather was bad and the road became impassable, he walked or wore snowshoes to work.

Katie was the accountant in the family and she saved every penny they didn't spend. She earned extra money selling eggs in town. Once in awhile someone would hear of her sewing ability and request she make them a dress. She crocheted beautiful baby sweaters and bonnets. They became quite popular too. She loved her chickens and slowly her brood increased until John had to build on to the chicken coop. Occasionally a hen would find its way into the stewing pot on a Sunday morning.

The Brokenstraw Creek flowed through the property on its way to the headwaters of the Allegheny River at Buckaloons.

The Buckaloons was the place where various Indian tribes used to meet to trade and camp back in the seventeenth century. The Brokenstraw began near a small Dutch village in western New York State known as Clymer. The water was cool and clear and was excellent for trout fishing. John would often grab a pole and spend a few hours catching a few fish for dinner. Sometimes Katie would join him and they would clean and cook the fish right on the riverbank.

Life was good for the young couple. Six months after they had moved into their home they found out they were going to become parents. They felt America had truly blessed them. Katie was sure it would be a boy who would look just like his father, but John felt it would be a beautiful baby girl, the picture of her mother. Seven months later they were pleased to announce they were the parents of twins! A boy and a girl! The boy they named Joseph Jan and the girl they christened Maria Theresa. The babies were born at the farm. It took awhile for Katie to recover, but soon she had them on a schedule. It was wonderful having the babies to keep her company all day when John was working. John built a wagon for the babies and Katie took them with her everywhere, to the garden, out to the barn, to the henhouse to collect the eggs, even to the pasture to round up the cows.

The very next summer Katie was pregnant again. This time it was a boy they named James Walter. Now Katie was busy with three children to take care of. Sewing clothes and making diapers took up a good deal of her time. Cooking, baking and taking care of the garden were other responsibilities. By the time she crawled into bed at night she was too tired to think of anything but trying to get a few hours of uninterrupted sleep.

Winter was an especially harsh time of year. The roads became impassable. There was nothing to do but stay inside the house and keep everyone warm and well. The woodstove was heating the house day and night. John had cut a lot of wood to see them through the winter. The woodshed was built close to the house, so that was a lifesaver when the blizzards came. Many mornings John would have to find his way to the barn by hanging on to a rope he had attached to the back porch all the way to the barn door.

Katie canned vegetables and fruit all summer. She bought peaches and apples and pears by the bushel and put them all in shiny jars which graced the many shelves in the fruit cellar. Jars of jellies also lined shelves along the walls. She baked bread daily and always had a pie or cake or cookies to treat John and the children.

The weeks before Christmas Katie stayed up late sewing clothes for a doll or knitting sweaters for John and the boys. John would be in the barn late at night hammering and sawing, making toys for the children. He would carve a horse and then make a wagon to go with it. Joseph would get a toy gun he had carved so he could go hunting with his papa.

John would travel into town and bring oranges and candy from the general store to put in each of their stockings. Christmas Day would bring cries of delight from each child as they discovered St. Nicolas had visited during the night. Katie would always find a special gift under the tree from John. He'd spend many hours making her a new wooden jewelry box or a cabinet for her clothes.

On nice Sundays they took the wagon into town to St. Thomas Catholic Church in the nearby town of Corry. Katie and John always had the babies baptized as soon as possible. The priest would bless them every Sunday as he knew how difficult it was to make it into town. Their faith kept them safe and happy and they were both very thankful for their children and for each other.

CHAPTER FIVE

THE FOLLOWING spring there was a new family to talk about in the valley. A lumber baron named Levi Clough was rumored to be buying up land nearby for the purpose of building a huge dairy farm. The cattle were reportedly coming all the way from Scotland! The barns were going to be the length of three barns put together. The house was rumored to be a castle. Everyone in the Spring Creek area was excited and anxious to see what would happen next.

The property under discussion was about two miles from the Wjotla farm. John didn't have much to say about it but Katie looked forward to meeting new neighbors. She was hoping they would have lots of children and the mother would be someone she could have as a friend. She pestered John to find out more information about the family, but John was reluctant to ask anyone. He liked to keep to himself and not be known as a gadabout.

He told her, "Katie, just be patient and wait. Levi Clough owns a lot of sawmills and logging operations in the Northwest. His uncle has furniture stores in the area and he suggested his nephew build a farm here in the valley. He wants to buy about fifteen hundred acres. That makes our one hundred sixty acres seem like nothing."

"I just hope they are a nice couple who have children. Joseph, Maria and James need more children to play and go to school with," remarked Katie.

The progress on the building of this showplace farm was slow but steady. The barns were huge. The silos and floor of the barns were constructed of concrete. Even the second story of the barns was hand-poured cement. All the cement had to be brought to the site and mixed by hand and then poured in sections. It was a tremendous undertaking and a miraculous feat back in the early 1900's.

The main house was going to be beautiful. It was three stories high and had a cellar and a summer kitchen in the back off the porch. The wallpaper had been ordered from Europe. There were eleven fireplaces!

Five other houses were built on the property to house the foreman and the workers needed to work the huge dairy operation.

Katie couldn't imagine a place like this in her corner of the world. She had seen castles in Poland. One castle she had seen as a youngster was the most famous castle in Poland. It was known as Lancut and was owned by Count Potocki. John and Katie came from simple people. Katie's family was considered middleclass citizens because they owned the land they farmed. Her great grandfather had shown incredible bravery in battle and in turn was given land by the king. They lived like peasants but they were a step above the serfs because they owned their land.

In truth there was no Poland. Poland as a country had been swallowed up by Russia, Austria and Prussia (Germany) in the latter part of the 18th century. This happened because Poland did not have a stable government or a dependable army.

Attempts were made to stamp out the history, the language, anything concerning Poland as an independent country. Austria was more German than Polish and Germany condescended to Russia so both countries took their frustrations out on Poland. The one problem with the Poles was they were under such rigid control of the Catholic Church. They had no freedom. They had never known democracy and what it was like to live free because they were always ruled by who ever chose to overtake their country and set up a governing party.

Both Katie and John had entered the United States as citizens from Polish Austria Galacia.

America to them was the land of milk and honey. Owning their own farm and being able to make their own decisions were things families in Poland could only dream about. John and Katie were determined to raise their family in a free society and never look back.

America was involved in a world war when the fourth child arrived in the Wjotla household. Martina Rose Wjotla joined Joseph, Maria and James late in 1918. That was the year America won the Great War and Poland was once again declared a free state after one hundred and twenty-three years of being divided.

Twin girls were born two years later. Marjorie Octavia and Irene Catherine were welcomed by their four siblings with great joy and their parents felt blessed by two healthy babies.

Six children were a lot to keep fed and clothed. John and Katie found it a simple task to supply each child with warm clothes in the winter. Shoes and coats were handed down from one to another, boy or girl not mattering in the least. Farm families gave willingly to their neighbors. They shared not only clothes and food but farm labor as well. Children shared rides to school and church and social events too. Neighbors were like family. You had to depend on each other to survive.

The closest town was five miles away. That was considered just a short stretch of the legs in the early 1900's. If you owned a horse or a wagon you were very fortunate.

When automobiles appeared on the scene it was indeed a reason to celebrate. It was a real treat to know someone who owned a car and an even bigger treat to be given a ride in one. It was a dress up affair but you didn't want to appear too hoity toity as you arrived at the church or store. Automobiles were not built for country roads after a rainstorm or blizzard. Horses were used to pull them out of the muck time and time again. If you were unlucky enough to go into a ditch you might be walking for awhile until you found someone to help get your vehicle back on solid ground.

CHAPTER SIX

B Y THE time Joseph and Maria started school in Spring Creek Township, the Clough Farm as it was known, was coming into completion as a "before its time" dairy operation in Northwest Pennsylvania.

Champion stock was shipped over to the States from as far away as Scotland. Red and white cattle soon dotted the landscape as far as one could see. The cattle had horns that were trained to grow a certain way, signifying to others that they were a breed known as Ayrshires.

The huge barn that accommodated these unique creatures had stanchions that included flooring made of wooden bricks to cushion the cow's legs as they weren't made to withstand the hard concrete floor.

The barns not only had concrete flooring, but floor-to-roof walks on both ends and two in the middle that separated the structure into fire-resistant areas. Tin-covered doors also acted as fire breaks.

The second floor of the two story barns was also made of poured concrete. There were no hay chutes from the loft to the ground floors. They could pose a fire hazard. Instead, hay was dropped into a separate middle area of the barn and carried to the cattle.

Straight, true, mammoth timbers crisscrossed the upper areas of both barns as roof supports. Tracks ran the length of both barns, from which large claws would lift and move the hay. There wasn't a crooked line in either barn.

Tracks above the milking area served two purposes, as barn cleaner moving manure out of the barn, and to move the milk cans neatly out the side of the barn to the milk house. It was there the milk was bottled before being shipped.

Spring Valley Farms was a modern dairy farm way before its time. Aside from being one of the foremost dairy operations in the country, Spring Valley Farms was also a retreat. Levi Clough was friends with a lot of America's industrial greats, such as Vanderbilt, Carnegie and Rockefeller. One of the primary lures was Spring Creek. Two miles of this creek ran through the Clough property.

Levi Clough was such a trout-fishing aficionado that he employed a game warden whose job focused solely on raising trout for stocking purposes, constructing in-stream gabions to create fishing pools, and monitoring the stream. Spring Creek was world renown as a premier site for fly fishing and sportsmen came from near and far to fish its waters. Local fisherman were not permitted to fish the creek on the Clough property.

Levi Clough never lived on the farm. He built a beautiful home in Warren, about twenty-five miles east of the property. The house was used for entertainment purposes at first and then was turned over to the farm manager as a residence. Katie was sad that she never got to meet Mrs. Clough nor their children.

Mr. Clough drove one of the first Peerless automobiles. He also startled the residents of Spring Creek when a new gasoline traction engine, or tractor, was unloaded at the Pennsylvania freight station. The local residents had never seen anything like it. It had the power of twenty horses.

John and Katie and their neighbors were fully aware that the wealth of Levi Clough far exceeded their own in terms of property and money. This was plainly apparent when the Clough Farm received the first electricity from an exclusive line from the village of Spring Creek supplied by Penn Electric. The electricity was used for lighting both the house and the barns and also for pumping water and running the washing machine! Farms and houses in the surrounding areas didn't have electricity until about twenty years later.

The village of Spring Creek only had about three hundred residents. There were two churches, a general store, a bank, the tannery and the blacksmith shop. The residents marveled at the huge farm that was built a little ways out of town. Because they were kept busy just trying to survive, they soon stopped paying attention to all the hoopla once it became routine. To them it was so extraordinary that it became a non-event. It didn't affect the way they lived or conducted business.

Joseph went to school with the son and daughter of the farm manager. He was invited to the house for a birthday party, or once in awhile just to spend the night with his friend. He would come home bursting with news about the "magical" house a few miles from his own. John and Katie would listen, assured he would forget about it in a few days as most boys do. He had his chores to do on the farm and they told him he was to be grateful he had a warm bed and food on the table and sisters and brother to play with.

One day Joseph rode into town with his father in the wagon to get some needed supplies. When they arrived in town there was a lot of commotion over near the railroad platform so John and Joseph walked over to see what was going on.

A crowd had gathered near one of the freight cars. A great deal of shouting was heard. Cries of pain intermixed with cursing and rage came pouring forth from the doorway of the boxcar.

A monster something was snorting and stomping and creating a ruckus from within the confines of its containment. Men began backing away and others just plain ran from the scene. John hoisted Joseph onto his shoulders and they took up a position behind some crates that had just been unloaded and stacked at the side of the freight building.

They first glimpsed the rope. It was a huge rope, the strands of which were as wide as a man's wrist. Three men were backing out of the railroad car, one with a chain as big around as a fist. At the end of that chain and rope being held by the three men stood a massive bull. It was red and white and it had huge horns on its gigantic head which must have measured two yards across. Snorting and bellowing it came out of the car, stomping its huge hooves and foaming at its mouth. The bull's eyes were wide with fright and confusion and anger at being pulled and yanked. The rope and chain were attached to a ring in the bull's nostrils.

"No wonder it's angry, Papa" said Joseph to his father. "It must really hurt bad to be pulled by your nose."

"Hush Joseph," cautioned his father. "That is one huge bull. I have never seen one quite that big before. I wouldn't be one of those men for all the tea in China!"

"Step back! Stand aside! Give us plenty of room here!" exclaimed a man walking quickly up the ramp to the train with a whip in his hand.

John quickly took Joseph from his shoulders and put him on the ground. "Joseph, I want you to stand over where you see William, the blacksmith and Frank from the general store. Stay right there until I come to get you." John spoke calmly, but with a voice Joseph had learned to obey and not question.

As Joseph watched from a safe distance his father walked right up to the man with the whip and stood in front of him blocking his path.

"What in tarnation do you think you are doing sir?" asked the indignant man, raising the whip to eye level with John.

Grabbing the whip and forcing it down along with the man holding it, John kept up the pressure until the man's grip was loosened and the whip dropped to the floor of the platform.

The crowd grew very quiet as John took the whip and threw it into a stand of weeds alongside the railroad tracks.

The man started to rise and John even helped him up, all the while holding on to the back of the man's shirt with one hand.

"This animal is frightened to death. Any idiot can see that. If anyone is hurt today it will be because of you and no one else! The last thing this bull needs is to be hit with a whip and become even more frenzied. Now get off this platform and stay off!"

"You'll be sorry mister!" the man threatened as he backed down the stairs to the street. Shaking his fist at John he kept retreating down the street. "Mr. Clough sent me to get his prized bull and he won't be happy with the likes of you….you foreigner!"

The crowd began murmuring among themselves and shaking their heads, some in agreement with the man and others supporting their friend, John Wjotla.

The men holding on to the wild and frightened bull weren't quite sure what had happened but were busy just trying to hold on for dear life before the monster pulled free and trampled them all to death.

John joined them in holding on to the chain and quietly began talking to the massive beast in hushed tones, at the same time staying away from the hooves that were thrashing about. He continued to speak softly, all the time keeping his eyes on the frightened eyes of the bull. Eventually he could feel the muscles of the animal relaxing a bit. His arms were totally exhausted from holding the chain so taut but slowly he and the other two men were able to pull the bull down the platform and toward the wagon. By the time they got the bull loaded they could barely stand. Their arms felt as though they had been pulled right out of their sockets.

Once the bull was safely loaded the crowd began to whoop and holler. They ran over and began slapping John on the back. Joseph came running over and jumped right into his father's arms.

"That was so brave of you, Papa!" he cried. "I thought for sure you were going to be killed!"

"Now Joseph, let this be a lesson to you" John exclaimed. "Never whip an animal or be unkind. You must be in control and then everything will be alright. Do you understand Joseph?"

"Yes, Papa" replied the boy, looking up at his father with new pride and respect.

"Mr. Wjotla! Hold up there a moment, sir!"

John and Joseph were just getting back in their wagon when John heard a man shout out his name. As he turned to see who was calling him, a gentleman in a huge top hat and fur coat was just alighting from one of those new gasoline-powered automobiles.

"Hello sir," the gentleman said with his hand outstretched to shake John's hand. "I am Levi Clough, the owner of Spring Valley Farms. I am proud to make your acquaintance! That bull is my most prized possession. I had him shipped all the way from Scotland. I want to thank you for helping with the unloading. I would not have been happy if something had happened to that bull after all I have gone through to get it here. It is a prize animal. I thank you kind sir!"

"Wow Papa".....Joseph started to say something but his father held up his hand for silence.

"Mr. Clough, a pleasure to meet you sir" replied John. "All I did was lend a helping hand. No thanks required. I just don't like to see an animal whipped."

"I don't either, Mr. Wjotla," said Mr. Clough. Especially an animal I paid a lot of money for! I could use a man of your talents on my farm. Would you consider coming to work for me?"

John held his restless horses in check while he smiled in reply to the lumber baron's offer. "Thank you very much, Mr. Clough. I appreciate your trust in me but I must decline. My wife, Katie, and our children have a small farm just north of yours and we are very happy there."

"Well, I can certainly understand that Mr. Wjotla, but if you ever need anything or if you like to fish, just contact my manager and tell him I said you and your family are welcome on my farm anytime and to give you anything you want!" With that said he climbed back into his vehicle and with a wave turned it around and headed back toward his farm, the cart with the prized bull following safely behind.

"Gee willikers Papa!" Joseph began again. "That was really Mr... Clough. Right, Papa? Wait until mama hears about this!"

"Now Joseph, we don't want to be worrying your mama," said John giving his son a hug. 'Let's just keep it our secret. Do you think you can do that?"

"Awww Papa, do I hafta keep it a secret? I can't tell anybody?" Joseph knew by his father's silence he would have to just let it go.

Joseph didn't tell his mother but that didn't matter. The whole township was talking about the incident for weeks. John was the new town hero for weeks before the gossip died down.

CHAPTER SEVEN

WHEN LEVI Clough began looking for his prized bull, the entire country of Scotland was turned upside down and inside out in an attempt to find the perfect bull. The bull Mr. Clough finally selected was out of what was "regarded by competent authorities as the greatest cow Scotland has produced." She was a heavy milker and of such outstanding individuality that she was unbeaten on the show yard, winning twenty-five firsts and the championship at leading Scottish exhibitions.

Levi Clough wanted people from every locality to see his magnificent Ayrshire herd. His farm now boasted over two hundred of the pure-bred red and whites.

Many hospitals, he would report, said that they had reached the conclusion that Ayrshire milk was indispensable in maintaining the health of their patients.

Spring Valley Farms eventually brought the herd to sufficient size to enable Mr. Clough to supply a large demand for superior milk. He built an up-to-date creamery at his farm. Every provision was made for handling the milk in a thoroughly sanitary manner from the time it left the cow until it reached the consumer.

The famous show herd of registered Ayrshire cattle from the Clough Farm traveled throughout the eastern United States winning many coveted prizes at various state fairs. The herd also took a number of grand championships. One such champion was listed as Primrose of Beaver Meadows Fourth, being the leader of the herd with an official record of 13,000 pounds of milk with a 4.7 butter fat test as a three year old.

The manager of the farm accompanied the herd along with up to ten handlers and various carloads of equipment as they made their trek from state to state.

Levi Clough tried many times to hire John Wjotla as the manager of Spring Valley Farms. One manager of the farm barely escaped being killed when he was attacked by the bull one evening. The incident occurred in the bull's stall. Mr. Seitz, the manager, was hurled to the floor and trampled upon. Other farmhands drove the bull off so Mr. Seitz could be rescued. He escaped with serious bruises. It took a special handler to take charge of that bull and John was Mr. Clough's first choice. John never took the job. He was content to manage his own farm and family.

Katie became friends with some of the wives of the farmhands who worked on the Clough farm. She heard all the gossip about the owner and his family. She was especially curious about the grand house. No one seemed to live in it very long.

One day Katie and the children were visiting Mrs. Bates who lived at the farm. Her husband was one of the teamsters who took care of the horses and was responsible for hauling the prized cattle from the barn to the railroad depot. Gramma Bates, as she was called, delighted in having the young Polish girl visit with her children. Joseph and James played with her grandsons who lived across the road. On this particular afternoon, Maria, Martina, Marjorie and Irene were playing with some hand-sewn dolls out on the grass under the huge maple tree in the front yard. Gramma Bates had made them each a doll so they would have something to play with each time they visited. Maria was busy sewing a dress for her doll. Her sisters kept begging her to make one for each of their dolls too.

Gramma Bates and Katie were sitting on the porch chatting and enjoying the beautiful warm day.

"Katie" exclaimed Gramma Bates, "I just had a wonderful idea. Let's take the girls and walk over to the main house. You have wanted to see it and today would be the perfect time since I am in charge of things around here."

"Oh Gramma Bates, could we really do that?"

"Why, we certainly can. Don't you worry your pretty little head about the boys. They're not the least bit interested in walking through that house. I'll just give a holler over there for Billy and Bobby to tell their momma where we're going and to keep her eye on them for a little while."

While Gramma Bates was doing that, Katie gathered the girls together and told them to put their dolls in the wagon.

"Where are we going, Mama?" asked Maria as she tugged gently on her mother's sleeve.

"Are we going home now mama?" sweet Martina inquired, looking up at her mama while holding her thumb in her mouth.

"Martina, please take your thumb out of your mouth, sweetie, when you're talking to mama. That's better, dumpling. Maria, take your sister's hand and bring Marjorie and Irene over here too."

Gramma Bates joined them as they waited in the yard. "Well young ladies" she directed as she pointed her arm toward the main house, "we are headed in that direction. We are taking a walk through the field over to the main house. We'll be quiet and ladylike and we won't make a sound, right?"

The four girls looked at each other and then up at their mother. "We promise we'll be very good mama" they chorused in agreement.

"I know you will be very good little girls" Katie said gently to her daughters. "This is a very fine house and we want to make a good impression and not cause any problems, so please don't touch anything!"

The girls all nodded so solemnly that both Katie and the older woman had to hide their smiles and chuckle.

The small group trudged up the front steps and waited while Gramma Bates unlocked the front door. Both entry doors had large oval windows with beveled glass designed in swirls with roses in the center. When they entered the vestibule they all uttered an "ooh" and then an "ahh" as they glimpsed for the first time the interior of the house.

Straight ahead was a gorgeous grand piano that looked magnificent sitting in the main living area. Flanked by a huge fireplace on one side and a very large palm-like plant on the other, it became the main focal point in the otherwise bare room. The wallpaper was brown with rose flowers trimmed in white and brown flowers trimmed in white and black. The piano was stark ebony with white keys and the effect was pure magic.

The parlor was filled with overstuffed chairs in rose velvet. A gigantic couch with brocade cushions covered in green and rose flowers took up one side of the room. The draperies were heavy velvet in a deep maroon with gold plaited tassels. Large tables in dark mahogany were scattered throughout the room. Tiffany lampshades balanced on tall lamps graced tables everywhere you looked.

As they made their way into the dining room, the first thing that drew their attention was the magnificent chandelier, which hung gracefully from the delicately sculpted ceiling. Row after row of crystal gems dangled from golden strands suspended from a cobalt blue center. The huge dining room table was beautiful. It was hand carved from dark cherry and the center was inlaid with gold stenciling and a rich painting of fruit and vines. The chairs had cushions made of blue brocaded material with gold threads running through the pattern. One entire wall was covered with shelves inside a massive cabinet that had a glass front four doors across. Inside was china which featured cobalt blue plates with an ivory center and gold filigree around the edges. Crystal glassware of every size and description graced the shelves. Crystal bowls, carafes and assorted dishes filled all the available space.

The children's eyes were as wide as saucers as they took in the opulence and grandeur. They had never seen anything like this in their short lives. They were used to crockery that didn't even match and wooden cupboards that often had a cotton cloth as a covering. They ate at a handmade table which often was covered with an oilcloth that could be wiped clean after a meal. Mama had a fancy tablecloth they used once or twice a year but nothing as fancy as this!

There was even an inside bathroom which was something the girls had never seen before. They marveled and giggled at the huge claw foot bathtub and when they saw the flush toilet they laughed and covered their faces in delight and embarrassment.

Gramma Bates reached over and turned the faucet on and when they saw water gushing out they put their little hands under the flow of water and giggled some more.

The stairs leading to the second floor and the newel posts supporting them were carved from dark cherry and were as solid as the tree that created them. The upstairs hallway was as wide as the girl's house. The master bedroom was huge. The massive bed was twice the size of Katie's and John's. An armoire covered one wall and a huge dresser with a mirror dominated the other. There was a big walk-in closet that would have enveloped both the girls' rooms at home.

The children's room had an alcove that held a bed with a canopy which thrilled the girls. They were all dreaming of actually having this fantasy come true at their house. Maria vowed then and there that someday her daughters would have a room just like this one!

The third floor was reached by a circular stairway that was very narrow and they had to ascend in single file. It had a door that opened to reveal one great room that was filled from end to end with bookshelves and toys. Doll carriages, child-sized tables, a spring horse, trucks, tricycles and wagons filled the room. The dolls were flung carelessly across the floor except for a shelf which contained porcelain dolls, beautifully dressed, with hair that begged to be brushed.

Marjorie reached up to touch one of the dolls but was stopped by her older sister who admonished her for even thinking of doing such a thing. Katie saw what was happening and immediately went forward and drew the children out of the room.

"I know what a temptation it is to want to play with all the toys and beautiful dolls, but we are guests in someone's home and we must respect their property," she cautioned, all the while wishing she hadn't brought them in the first place. It was all too much for a small child to comprehend. Like Christmas in a toy store, life could be so disappointing to a child. She didn't want her daughters to feel badly because they didn't have all these wonderful things.

The last room they visited was the kitchen. A double fireplace with hanging pots of every shape and size filled one wall. Made from local stone, the fireplace loomed enormous although the kitchen was very large. A massive stove occupied one wall with an icebox next to it. A solid maple table with eight chairs sat off to one side. It was adorned with a lazy susan in the middle with colorful salt and pepper shakers in the shape of roosters on it along with a sugar bowl and matching creamer. An empty milk bottle which had Spring Valley Farms printed across the front lay on its side.

They exited the house through the back door which also had a screen door attached. The back porch led to a summer kitchen which also had a stove and oven and shelves of dishes and glassware and kitchen utensils.

By the time they finished they were all exhausted. They trudged back to Gramma Bates house to enjoy a glass of lemonade and some freshly baked cookies before gathering the boys and heading back up the hill to their home.

The children chattered the entire way as the girls excitedly described what they had seen to their brothers, especially the playroom. Joseph and James just wanted to talk about the fort they had built with the Kafferlin twins so everyone was talking at once. Katie just smiled and continued walking, occasionally picking Irene or Marjorie up and walking with them as she thanked the Lord for their health and boisterousness. One thing she hadn't experienced in the house she toured today was happiness. It had contained many beautiful things but none of them replaced the feeling of warmth and love she felt every day in her little cottage.

By the time they entered their yard, the children were dragging from their very busy day so Katie made them all go inside and take a short nap before chores had to be done. She rested awhile too and when she awoke she was amazed to see it was almost dark outside. She hurriedly woke the sleeping children and hustled them out the door to feed the chickens and bring the cows in for milking.

Goodness, she thought, John will be home any minute and she hadn't even started supper. She decided some scrambled eggs and smoked sausage would be a good start and it would be quick to fix. She grabbed a skillet and began breaking eggs into it. She then chopped some onions and green pepper. As she took a minute to step outside to retrieve the meat from the smokehouse, she noticed a strange glow in the sky off to the east. The village of Spring Creek was in that direction. The wind had picked up a bit and the clouds were moving in so she knew they were in for a little rain. She began to wonder why John wasn't home. She called the children and brought them into the house. The older girls helped with preparations for supper.

She and the children ate by themselves that night. After doing the dishes and getting the children washed and into their night-clothes, Katie again wandered outside to look down the road to see if John was coming. Joseph followed her outside. He too saw the reddish glow off in the distance.

"It looks like a fire to me mama" he said, stretching his neck to try and see beyond the hill."

"Oh dear, Joseph. Do you suppose your papa is helping a farmer fight a barn fire?"

"If there is a fire, papa will be there helping," replied her young son. "Papa is the bravest man on earth, mama!"

"The wind will bring the rain shortly," Katie remarked matter-of-factly. 'That should bring an end to the fire quickly."

They went back inside. The children played a game of hide the button before being read a story and going off to bed. Katie tucked each one in and kissed them goodnight.

"Will papa be home soon, mama?" James asked as she placed his cloth horse into his outstretched hands.

"Yes, darling, Papa will be here any minute. You just close your eyes and the minute he gets home he will come in and kiss them asleep. Goodnight sweet prince."

"Goodnight Mama" sounded the voices of all six children as

they said their prayers and pulled their covers up and snuggled down in their beds.

Katie cleaned the kitchen, picked up the clothes and began making bread for the next day. She was getting very worried about John. They didn't have a telephone or even a radio. She would just have to be patient. As the hours went by and John didn't come home she felt as though she just had to do something!

Wrapping her shawl around her shoulders she sprinted out to the barn and climbed the stairs up to the hayloft. Throwing open the doors to the outside of the second story she gazed off in the direction of the light. It was definitely a fire, she surmised. The sky was hazy with smoke and she could smell it as it drifted over the hill.

She went down the ladder, grabbed a lantern off the post in the tack room and went back to the loft to watch for John.

Soon the sound of raindrops was heard plunking on the tin roof. Katie thanked God for that because it meant the fire would soon be out and John would be home.

As the time passed, Katie thought of her life in Poland and the new life she had in America. She wished her parents could see her home and meet their grandchildren. They would be so happy to know she was okay and doing so well. She thought of John and what a wonderful husband and father he was. I don't know what I would do if something happened to him, she pondered. Please come home, John, she prayed silently.

John was coming across the hill. He was exhausted and drained, his horse hungry and tired. When he looked up he thought he saw a light coming from the direction of his farm. Yes, it was a light! He could see the silhouette of Katie standing at the door of the hayloft with a lantern held high as she searched the darkness through the pouring rain looking for him.

Katie was straining to see if she had perhaps seen a figure coming over the hill. Could it be.....yes, it was John and his horse, Ben. Did he just wave? It was John! She almost tripped over her own feet as she raced to the ladder and began her descent down the steps.

She waited at the doorway to the barn as John and Ben drew closer and closer. The rain was coming down in torrents now. As they drew closer she could see her husband was covered in ashes and soot. His hair was plastered against his forehead. He looked exhausted and spent. She was sure he was chilled to the bone. She had never loved him as much as she did at this moment.

John didn't have to do much to get old Ben into the barn. The horse was beyond tired from standing outside all day and then again practically all night in the rain without being brushed down or fed. He headed straight to his stall and began munching on some hay.

John approached Katie and took the lantern from her hand and set it on the shelf. He didn't say a word and hushed her as she started to open her mouth to speak. He held her in his arms for a long time before holding her away from him and looking into her face. Their eyes met and she saw anguish and torment reflected in them. Without uttering a word his lips came down on hers and she experienced the most passionate kiss she had ever received. He was drenched and so was she, her hair plastered all over her face, her dress clinging to every curve of her body. To John she was the most beautiful creature ever created. Lust merged with passion as they dropped down into the hay grasping at each other as if seeing each other for the first time. Their bodies couldn't get enough of each other as they ravenously devoured the other in their quest to end this seemingly out of control, endless hunger and need for each other. They climaxed simultaneously and continued to hold each other tightly as they both fought to regain control.

John arose first and helped Katie up from the floor and they began brushing hay off each other as they tried not to laugh at how silly they both looked. They were like two scarecrows standing outside the entrance to the barn hugging each other and dancing around in the rain. Together they walked to the house, their hands and fingers entwined.

Later, they sat in the kitchen having a cup of coffee and a late night snack. John told her about the events of the day and exactly what had happened at the tannery.

"It was a nightmare Katie," he related excitedly. "One minute I was gathering my things to leave work for the day and head home and the next flames were whipping about my face. I had to run out as fast as I could. I ran over to Ben and led him away from the burning building. That place went up so fast no one could have saved it."

"My goodness! How horrible that must have been! Was anyone hurt or killed?" Katie held her one hand to her throat and reached out to cover John's hand with her other hand.

"No one knows for sure, but it would be a miracle if no one was killed. The fire spread so quickly. The tannery is completely destroyed. We were lucky it began to rain or we could have lost half the town of Spring Creek."

"You're exhausted John. Let's go to bed and try to get some sleep. The children will be up in a few hours. We'll talk about it in the morning."

"You're right Katie. You go on to bed. I'm going to check on Ben and make sure he is put away for the night. He inhaled a lot of smoke and I need to make sure he's okay."

Katie washed their few dishes and put them on the towel to dry. She had taken a bath and shampooed her hair so she was ready to fall into bed and sleep for hours.

John finally came in and slipped out of his clothes. He had washed up in the barn and smelled like soap and leather. He gave a sigh as he crawled into the other side of the bed. He held tightly to Katie. In just a few minutes he was snoring. Katie was so grateful he was home safe and sound. They both fell into a deep sleep and didn't awaken until the children came in wondering why there wasn't any breakfast ready!

Katie and John knew their relationship had changed that night. It almost seemed like they had discovered each other anew. After fourteen years of marriage their lives had just taken a turn for the better. They found it difficult to keep their hands off each other. This is how God works his magic in people's lives. He drives a lightning bolt straight through their hearts.

Nine months to the day after the fire, John Tanner Wjotla made his way into the world as wild as the passion under which he had been conceived. He looked just like his mother but his eyes were as deep a green as his father's. He was soon the apple of everyone's eye. His brothers and sisters adored him and couldn't do enough to see that he was content and loved. He hardly ever cried or made a fuss. He was a very loving child and was extremely outgoing.

As he grew older he was quite a handful. He had absolutely no fear. One day the family was shocked to find him atop the barn roof. As John ran to get a ladder, Katie watched in horror as her young son grasped the hook that brought the hay up to the loft and swung out over the barn yard and back into the open door of the hayloft. For that feat he received a sound spanking from his father. Katie was also angry at this foolish and dangerous caper. They were all thankful he wasn't hurt. His brothers and sisters made a pact that they would certainly be keeping a closer eye on their younger brother.

CHAPTER EIGHT

THE 1920's was an extremely volatile period in the Midwest and the eastern United States. Change provokes anxiety and anxiety in turn provokes fear and many people capitalize on fear.

Prohibition was a mistake to begin with. Prohibition was the eighteenth amendment to the United States Constitution. It was called The Volstead Act, which was passed on October 10th, 1919. This Act outlined that it was illegal to import, export, transport, sell, manufacture, barter and own any beverages which contained more than 0.5% alcohol excluding the alcohol used for medicinal and sacramental purposes.

The main purpose of Prohibition was to reduce crime, poverty, death rates, tax burden created by prisons and poorhouses, improve health and hygiene in America, solve social problems and improve the economy and quality of life. The government, even though they passed the law, did not fund well for this almost impossible undertaking. This Act increased homicide in large cities by 78%. The number of people incarcerated increased 561%.

Because Canada had repelled their Prohibition on the sale of alcohol a few years before, gangsters like Al Capone in Chicago created huge export companies smuggling illegal alcohol across the border into the United States. Barely 5% of illegal alcohol was caught being smuggled into the country.

An average of two thousand people a year died from drinking

liquor made from industrialized alcohol that never had the poisonous additives removed.

In the beginning the consumption of alcohol did decrease because the price of imported alcohol was so high. It also solved social problems for a time because men weren't drinking and thus the abuse of women and children decreased.

Crime soon increased because of the emergence of gangsters like Al Capone. New York City alone had over one hundred thousand speak-easies at the height of the Prohibition era.

Prohibition lasted thirteen years and it ended up causing more harm than good. Law enforcement officials were never successful in persuading the government to mount a wholehearted campaign against illegal suppliers of beverage alcohol. It was a lost cause from the beginning. President Franklin D. Roosevelt finally repelled Prohibition by passing the 21st amendment in 1933.

During the Prohibition years John was working nights at the Corry Radiator Company in Corry. He often noticed trucks and cars on his road as he was coming home. These were vehicles he didn't recognize and because he knew his neighbors schedule and what vehicles they drove, he was very suspicious of what was going on in the wee hours between darkness and dawn.

John didn't have anything against people drinking or making their own alcoholic beverages. He and other men in the area often made homemade beer for social events. They never sold it or attempted to profit from it.

Most lawmen looked the other way and ignored the small moonshining operations. On the other hand, if a large bootlegging operation was discovered and shipments were being made by less than legal means, then that became a different matter entirely.

The problems arose when the criminal element found in the

big cities, descended upon the rural communities, hence causing conflict and sometimes promoting grievous harm to the local
citizens.

John had heard rumors of a moonshining ring operating out
of Jackson Rocks up on Jackson Hill. Jackson Hill was about a
mile up the road from the Clough Farm. John reasoned that in
this era of Prohibition, the Sickler brothers were running their
moonshine operation up in the rocks. The Sicklers had a farm
right next to Jackson Rocks and they always had a still going back
in the woods.

Apparently, they were bringing the moonshine down the hill by
wagon and making the transfer to the bootleggers at the Clough
Farm. The rum runners would then head to Buffalo, Pittsburgh
and Cleveland and sell it to the organized crime groups that were
operating along the east coast and into the Midwest.

Levi Clough had passed away in 1927 after a long illness. The
farm continued to operate but soon the Ayrshire cattle were sold
and the farm sat idle for many years. The beautiful barns sat empty.
The house had several occupants who lived there for awhile and
then disappeared. The caretaker's houses fell into disrepair and
the place became a haven for nere do wells and vagrants.

It was a perfect place for rumrunners to congregate and distrib-
ute their illegal alcohol.

John didn't care that the Sickler brothers were making moonshine and selling it, but he did have a problem with strangers with
guns racing up and down the back roads putting his family at risk
and disturbing the livestock.

One Saturday John and his neighbors met with the local law
enforcement at the Spring Creek Grange to discuss the problem.
It was soon after this meeting that a nighttime raid was conducted
at the Clough farm and another up at Jackson Rocks. That ended

the problem in Spring Creek Township.

John and his neighbors were greatly relieved when prohibition ended. The back roads were quiet. Strange men carrying tommy guns and driving trucks were no longer seen hanging around the Clough farm. Local familie's fears were reduced. The community returned to normal. Moonshining still took place but it was kept at the local level.

CHAPTER NINE

ENTERTAINMENT WAS scarce in the years between the two World Wars. Life on the farm was hard work. From sun up to sun down the days were filled with chores. You not only had work inside the house but outside in the garden. Plus you had to take care of the livestock and projects in the barn and out in the fields. The landscape surrounding Spring Creek in the Brokenstraw Valley was dotted with hundreds of small farms. Many immigrants from Eastern Europe made their way to the valley to settle and raise their families. The census of 1930 was full of unusual names, some very difficult to pronounce. Names like Kratkowski, Wesoloski, Stavros, Wocienewsz, Toplovich and Thomco. The residents were a tightly knit group. Most were Roman Catholic. Their church was their common bond and many of the events in their lives centered around the church.

Weddings and funerals offered a place to get together and socialize. A wedding was an especially wonderful occasion to get together and see old friends. Months were spent planning the event. Bridal showers were held a few months prior to the wedding day. It wasn't unusual for two hundred people or more to be invited and attend.

Weddings provided the perfect opportunity for the younger people to meet each other and develop new relationships.

The Great Depression did not affect the small farmers in the valley very much. Life went on pretty much as usual. Joseph and

James helped on the farm while John continued to work in town at Corry Radiator. The boys tended the livestock and did most of the planting and harvesting. John did butchering on the side and also was good at wallpapering. He was a valuable asset to his family, neighbors and friends.

The children walked the eight miles into town at least once a week. They all studied catechism and celebrated their first communion at Saint Thomas Catholic Church. The population in Corry had swelled to over six thousand people. The railroad was the center of its existence. Many trains ran through the center of town at all hours of the day and night. It was one of these trains that emitted the spark that caused the devastating fire at the tannery in Spring Creek. Following that debacle, no new factories were permitted to be built next to the railroad tracks unless it was constructed of brick or concrete.

In 1932 John Wjotla purchased his first automobile. The family was very proud of their new possession. At last they too could drive into town and not have to waste time walking or hitching up the horses to a buggy or wagon. It wasn't a brand new car but to the Wjotlas, it was priceless.

One summer day the Wjotla family received an invitation to Etta Royek's wedding. Etta was the oldest daughter of Walter Royek, John's best friend. They lived at the top of South Center Street hill in Corry. The wedding was going to be attended by a lot of their friends and relatives in the area.

Katie was kept very busy making new dresses for herself and her daughters and new shirts for John and the boys. John Tanner would be wearing dress pants for the first time in his young life.

Katie was often perplexed by her youngest son's behavior. He was never still and if he was you just knew something was about to happen in the Wjotla household. John had told her not to worry. He said John Tanner was just headstrong and fearless.

"Ya" she would reply, "That's what I'm afraid of."

Katie found some blue material with pink rosebuds at the general store. She decided it would be the perfect color for a dress to wear to the wedding. Maria had her heart set on some yellow material she found at the Woolworth Store in Corry. She was working part time for the doctor's wife in Spring Creek cleaning house. She bought the material and sewed most of the dress herself.

Martina wasn't sure what color to pick for her dress. She was very independent and wanted something no one else would have. She was becoming a very lovely young lady. She wanted to be noticed and recognized as her own person. She finally settled on a lavender material with silver threads running through the fabric. She also decided upon a different pattern. Katie just shook her head and promised to try her best.

The twins, Marjorie and Irene always wanted to be dressed exactly alike. They liked anything in pink. Katie always added a ruffle or two to go with their curly hair and sweet round faces.

Luckily they all found shoes at the church rummage sale. It wasn't often that farm folks could afford new shoes for everybody. Katie had offered to help with the church sale so she could get a first look at the merchandise as it came into the church basement. She found shoes for the boys as well. Joseph was wearing the same size as his father. James's shoes were a tad too large but they would do. He would soon grow into them. John Tanner would be wearing his first pair of oxfords. He was having a fit about that!

The day of the wedding dawned sunny and warm. It was perfect for a ride into town to the church and then on up the hill to the Royek farm for the reception and celebration. Katie packed blankets and pillows for everyone because they would be spending the night. They would bed down in the wagon or on the ground. The car wouldn't be big enough to sleep everyone.

John Tanner was cautioned to behave and not do anything crazy when he got with all the young boys his age. He was not to bother the chickens or create havoc in the barn. Most importantly, there was to be no horseplay during the wedding mass!

When the family arrived at the church they eagerly greeted friends they hadn't seen in a very long time. The girls went off with their friends admiring each other's dresses and giggling over the attention of the boys who stood off to one side trying to pretend they were ignoring all the goings on but actually looking each girl over to see which one they would like to approach when the dancing began later that day.

The bells began ringing announcing the wedding was about to begin, so everyone began entering the church. John and Katie took a pew toward the rear of the sanctuary so they could easily make their escape should John Tanner become restless and begin misbehaving. John sat next to him with Joseph on the other side. Katie had brought a few treats to keep him occupied and quiet. The older children knew that punishment would be swift and severe if any disrespect was shown inside the church.

The bride looked radiant on the arm of her father as she glided down the aisle of the church. The groom was a Polish boy who lived in a community about fifteen miles from Corry. He worked in one of the factories in the area. The couple would be setting up housekeeping in Corry. Katie had toured the apartment with the bride's mother and thought it was very suitable for a newly married couple.

The church looked quite lovely that morning. It was built of brick and was one of the largest in that part of the country. It boasted a Catholic school from grades one through eighth. The church averaged two weddings a weekend in the summer months. The congregation was numbering close to 400 members which was a lot in the 1930's.

The wedding mass lasted about an hour. Surprisingly, John Tanner behaved quite admirably except for one brief moment when a pea shooter appeared. The recipient of the expelled pea literally jumped out of his seat when the propellant hit him square in the back of the neck. Joseph quickly removed the weapon from his brother's hands and put it in his pocket before his parents were aware of who had been the offender.

The vows were exchanged and soon everyone had departed the church. The guests were waiting on the steps for the newly wedded couple to appear. Everyone was given a handful of rice. Already some of the rice had been thrown by a few errant youngsters.

The bride and groom eventually emerged from the church and everyone yelled their congratulations and threw the rice on the couple as they hurried down the steps and disappeared into the back of an automobile. The groom had recently purchased a new car and was proudly showing it off on his wedding day.

Flowers were thrown at the car as it departed the parking lot. More rice was tossed and best wishes were heard until the car disappeared from sight.

Everyone got into their vehicles, wagons, and buggies and began the ascent up the hill to the Royek farm. It made quite a caravan as it wound through the streets of Corry and on up to the top of the hill.

Joseph and Maria had asked if they could ride with some of their friends. After receiving permission from their parents they happily trotted off to join other young people their age in making the trek to Etta's home. John Tanner was put on the seat between his parents. His three sisters sat in the back seat. James drove the wagon so the family could sleep in the back that night. Martina, Marjorie and Irene were all excited about the wedding. They discussed every detail on the way to the reception.

When they arrived at the farm, they were directed where to park the car. James unhitched the horses and led them to the barn to be brushed down before being put out to pasture for the duration of their stay. John unloaded the food they had brought while Katie carried the quilt she had made as a wedding gift for the couple into the house to be placed with the other gifts.

John Tanner ran off to play with the other little boys and girls who were racing around the yard chasing the dogs. It was good for them to release all that pent up energy. They would soon tire of chasing the dogs and then the chasing each other would begin.

Martina, Maria and Katie were helping Mrs. Royek set the tables and put out the food. Marjorie and Irene put the silverware out and filled the punchbowls. Other ladies sliced the meats and the bread and brought out platters of cold cuts. A few of the men formed a polka band and brought out their fiddles and accordions. Soon the entire homestead was awash with people, including running children, and the air was filled with joyous and happy music.

The men congregated near the beer kegs, swapping stories and lies. They kept their ears tuned for the cry that dinner was ready.

The tables were groaning under the weight of all the food. Platters of beef and pork and chicken, bowls full of sauerkraut and kielbasa, pierogies and halupkies. Salads of every kind, fruit salads, cucumbers and onions, coleslaw, bean salad, potato salad and macaroni salad too. Vegetables, including fresh carrots and string beans sat inviting on the tables. Breads of every variety, carefully arranged in baskets awaited the choice of each guest.

The wedding cake remained on the porch. It was a delightful

creation, five layers high with fresh flowers decorating the top tier. Fresh strawberries encircled the base of the cake, with more hiding under the frosting between layers of cream filling. The children were warned several times to stay clear of the area until after the cake cutting was concluded.

Katie had already put out the word to the older children to make sure John Tanner never came closer than twenty feet from the porch!

The guests ate until they couldn't swallow another bite. The bride and groom retired to the house for a much needed nap. The men began setting up tables for playing cards while the women cleared the tables and washed the multitude of dishes and silverware. Young children were encouraged to nap, but that didn't necessarily happen.

The teenagers went their own way, some changing clothes and getting together a game of softball or croquet. They broke into groups, some playing a quiet board game or just chatting.

After the kitchen was straightened, Katie and the other women got their embroidery or sewing or knitting and found a nice shade tree to sit under and gossip the afternoon away.

When the sun began to set over the hill the newlyweds appeared from the house to the sounds of clapping and guffaws and whistles. This was the signal for the gifts to be brought out and opened. A few of the tables were cleared to display the gifts once they had been opened.

All the little girls wanted to sit right up front so they wouldn't miss any of the proceedings as they whispered and giggled about everything the bride and groom did. Every time they kissed the little girls would titter and point and collapse in laughter.

All little girls dreamed of their wedding day and imagined who their prince would be. Certainly not any of the boys they were playing with today! Goodness no!

The boys wanted nothing to do with opening presents. They considered that a "girl" thing. They were content in looking for bugs in the fields or tadpoles in the farm pond.

Katie latched on to John Tanner as he passed her by at a full gallop and pulled him down beside her on the grass.

"Sit awhile with mama, John Tanner" she pleaded, sitting him down on her lap.

"Aw mama, let me go" struggled the youngster, squirming out of her reach and jumping up and running across the yard.

"Let him go, Mama," implored the twins as they watched him scamper off to join his friends. "Let him run and play so we can enjoy the peace and quiet!"

Everyone around them laughed and agreed. "He'll be fine, Katie, don't worry about the boy!" They all knew how protective Katie was of her youngest son. Katie just smiled and nodded in agreement.

Etta and her new husband, Harry, loved the quilt Katie had made. They proudly displayed it by hanging it from the bough of a tree in the front yard so everyone could admire it.

The gifts were soon opened and displayed on the tables. Everyone walked around the tables looking at everything. Etta and Harry walked through the yard full of guests thanking everyone for their generosity. With the help of several of the men, the gifts were transferred to the porch so more tables could be set up for the evening meal. It was nonstop eating at events like these. The women laughed as they trotted out of the house carrying the dishes they had just washed a few hours before. Now they were starting the same process over again.

Some of the men were too far gone from an afternoon of drinking to join the line for another helping of food. Most of the wives took care to make sure they fixed their husbands a plate of food to offset the beer and the whiskey.

After dinner it would be time to cut the cake and then the music would start and the dancing would begin. Everyone would then collapse in exhaustion and call it a day.

Katie rounded up her family and made them all eat a little something. John Tanner was told to settle down and take a plate of food and sit with his brothers and sisters. James scolded him for bringing a frog to the table and scaring the twins. John Tanner said he was sorry but he was already thinking what he could do with the frog when he found it again.

The skies were dark when the tables were finally cleared for the second time that day and the food was once again packed away. Lanterns had been hung from the tree limbs and also from the porch ceiling so everyone could see where they were going and what was taking place. The lines to the privy were long even though Walter had put up another outhouse to accommodate all his guests. Everyone was anxious to get back and join the activities as soon as possible.

The band began to play a lively polka and it wasn't long before everyone was up dancing or sitting and singing along with the band. When babies and young children fell by the wayside fast asleep their parents would tuck them in under a blanket out of harm's way and continue to dance and enjoy the party.

The party was about to come to a close when everyone was startled at the sight of a huge flaming cross which just seemed to appear out of nowhere on top of the hill behind the house. As everyone stared at the spectacle of the burning cross, their mouths gaping in shock and wonderment, over and down the hill came a dozen or more riders on horseback. As they neared the front yard, everyone could see they were wearing long white robes with hoods and eye holes cut out so all you could see were their eyes. The hoods came to a point on top. No one had ever seen such a sight before. They were frightened at this violent intrusion. Parents stood in front of their children, protecting them from whatever danger these men presented.

Even their horses were covered in white sheeting with just their eyes showing, as they pawed the ground and snorted and whinnied.

Everyone was too stunned to speak, but finally John walked toward the horse upon whose back sat the leader of the group of horsemen.

"What the hell is going on here?" demanded John, as other men joined him looking up at the horseman.

"Stay right where you are!" commanded a voice from under the hood. "You take a good look at that cross burning up on that hill! That will soon be your houses, you worthless bunch of Catholic immigrants! We don't want your kind in our valley! Go back to your own damn country and get out of ours, you bunch of stupid Polacks!"

Before John or any of the other men could respond, young John Tanner came running toward the horseman, legs a' churning as fast as he could until he stopped right in front of the startled leader. John Tanner's eyes were just ablaze and his little chest was heaving as he paused to catch his breath.

"Mister, don't you call my father a no-good Polack, you stupid bunch of halloweeners!" he shouted, running up and throwing a rock at the leader of the horsemen.

John and Joseph ran up and hauled the boy away just as the horseman was about to strike him with a whip he had tied to his saddle.

"Get that worthless whelp away from me before I lay his hide open with this whip!" threatened the leader as he calmed his horse and retreated a few steps. The other horsemen had pulled out rifles and pistols and were murmuring among each other.

"Don't ever threaten my boy again, you worthless piece of human scum!" shouted a very angry John Wjotla, striding toward the group of horsemen with most of the angry farmers, relatives and friends following behind, some picking up pitchforks and shovels or chairs or anything else they could find as weapons.

The horsemen began pointing their guns into the air and shooting at the sky. Screams filled the air as the women raced to get their children and get them out of the area. They had never been so frightened.

Katie grabbed John Tanner before he could do anything stupid and raced with him and the girls to the safety of the house.

Just as quickly as they had arrived the horsemen turned their horses and galloped off into the darkness. The cross continued to burn until it was just a charcoaled blackened skeleton of wood.

The chaos at the farm continued as everyone began talking at once. The children's cries were soothed and soon everyone settled down and began to comfort those who were shaken and weeping from fright.

Most who lived close by gathered their families and headed home, wanting the safety of their own beds and the men wanting the protection of their guns.

John and Katie opted to spend the night with their friends. They did not want to be caught out on the open roads, and they felt they shouldn't abandon their friends should the sheeted cowards return.

It took awhile, but Katie managed to calm John Tanner down and get him settled for the night on the floor in the living room. She promised him she would be sleeping right next to him and so would his brothers and sisters. John would sleep outside under the wagon with Joseph. He wasn't alone. The men who remained slept outside, their weapons at the ready. Even the bridegroom was there, next to his father and new father-in-law. They were ready this time. None of them got any sleep as the night sky soon turned to the light of dawn.

In the morning those who stayed helped to clean up the mess left by the chaos and one by one the families packed their things and departed for their own homes and farms. Walter and Bess thanked them all for coming and helping. They discussed ideas of what to do about the men who invaded their private party the night before and interrupted the celebration so violently. They decided to notify the State Police and have them conduct a full investigation.

The local papers reported the incident the following day. The unexpected guests at the wedding reception were described as being members of the local chapter of the emerging Ku Klux Klan, a radical vigilante organization. This organization based their philosophy on white supremacy and was intensely anti-Semitic and anti-Catholic. They preyed upon the immigrant population and tried to scare them by fear and coercion.

Founded in 1866 in Pulaski, Tennessee, the organization was first led by a Civil War veteran, General Nathan Forrest. The members dressed in white robes and white headdresses and rode horses covered with white robes. The horse's hooves were also muffled by cloth boots. Skulls adorned their saddle horns and they posed as dead Confederate soldiers returning from the fields of battle. They preyed upon black insurgents, carpetbaggers and scalawags who flooded the South at the end of the Civil War.

In 1869 General Forrest disbanded the KKK because even he felt the leadership was becoming too abusive of power and were getting out of hand with the use of terror.

The Ku Klux Klan continued to operate without his leadership and soon became a major terror organization in the south. In 1915, William Simmons, an ex-minister and promoter of fraternal organizations re-established the movement of the KKK by adding "white supremacy" to its agenda.

By the 1920's and 1930's the Klan numbered over 250,000 in Northwestern Pennsylvania. Its hatred extended to recent immigrants of Eastern European descent who settled in the valleys of several counties in northwestern Pennsylvania. The Klan stressed fundamentalist religion and despised Catholics and Jews. Their cross burnings and midnight rides spread terror throughout the countryside.

Many of the Klansmen were respected citizens in their communities. Staunch Protestants, they were role model citizens by day and turned into ugly terrorists at night. Too often judges and local politicians turned a deaf ear to their antics and, because of indifference, the KKK continued to thrive.

Many towns in northwestern Pennsylvania employed immigrants to work the coal mines. The small towns that sprung up were largely predominantly Catholic and also were strongholds for the United Mine Workers Union.

The Union had a history of firing known Klan members and was thus often targeted by the Klan.

In 1924 a large number of Ku Klux Klansmen rode the train to Lilly, Pennsylvania, a small mining town in Cambria County. They marched down the main street of town carrying guns and threatening the innocent citizens of that community. They shut off the electricity and left the town in darkness.

The Klan erected and burned crosses at the top of the hill in the center of town. As quickly as the crosses were erected the townspeople tore them down. They chased the Klan out of their town by turning fire hoses on them. Both townspeople and Klansmen were killed that night but at least the citizens of Lilly made their point in standing up against this evil force of hate. It may have been the turning point in the fall of the KKK in the Northeast.

The sad point of the era of the KKK was Protestant children were told not to associate with Catholic children and vice-versa. This distrust continued for several years and became an underlying factor in the politics of many towns.

John and Katie did their best to speak to their children about the KKK. They didn't understand it themselves but they did know about persecution and anarchy. Their children were instructed to stand up to fight a wrong. Don't be silent in their classrooms or when it was time to vote in an election. Speak out for what is morally right and defend the candidate who is trying to do what's best for the people.

CHAPTER TEN

JOHN TANNER never forgot that night at the Royek farm. It was his first taste of hate and bigotry and he didn't like the feeling. He changed that night and became very protective of his family and friends. He was threatened that night by something he didn't understand.

By the time he turned ten years old, John Tanner Wjotla was one of the brightest kids in the township. He had been advanced a grade in school and was very good at observing and absorbing everything that went on around him.

His classmates began to call him JT and the nickname stuck. He didn't mind the new name and it gave him a separate identity from his father.

JT knew the Ku Klux Klan still was active in their valley. He had seen their crosses burning at their meeting house at the top of Piccadilli Hill. An abandoned schoolhouse sat at the top of the hill and it was there they gathered to shoot their guns and dance around and speak in a strange language known only to Klansmen. They drank alcohol and shouted epithets and behaved like crazed lunatics.

JT could not understand why the KKK felt such hatred toward the Poles, Germans, Slavs and other immigrants from Eastern Europe. They were considered good, hard-working people. They were in America searching for a life of freedom and the chance to live a better life. They upheld the laws and were active in community service. He vowed he would always stand up against those few who initiated fear and terror among the innocent.

JT was twelve when he heard in school that the KKK had kidnapped the granddaughter of a judge in Pittsburgh in their attempt to buy a verdict for one of their members who was standing trial for murder. The member just happened to be a Grand Imperial Wizard, the highest rank in the Klan. The judge was a popular legalist and was known to be anti-KKK. Things were not going well for the indicted and something had to be done to influence the court.

A few KKK members kidnapped the judge's granddaughter as she was returning home from school. The girl had lived with her grandparents ever since her parents were killed in a skiing accident in Colorado. The police were looking for the child all over the state. Fliers were posted in all the post offices and local law enforcement was told to be extra cautious when approaching any known Klan members in their community.

John brought the news of the kidnapping up at dinner one night. The KKK was always a topic in the Wjotla household because of what had happened at the Royek wedding. They had never experienced any further trouble from the KKK but they were always alert and suspicious of many men they did business with in town.

By the time of the kidnapping, Joseph, Maria, James and Martina were all living in town. Joseph was working at the filling station and Maria was a housekeeper for the owner of one of the large manufacturing companies. James spent all his time helping the local vet. Martina worked part time for a local attorney. Marjorie and Irene were excellent seamstresses and always had plenty of offers to open their own shop. They wanted to get married and travel the world so they saved every penny they made.

Many of the children's friends were doing the same, living in town and attending school, working at night and then going home on weekends to help out on the farm. During school vacations they helped with the harvesting and canning. It was the only solution to being able to go to high school to complete their education.

JT still spent a lot of time at the Clough farm even though it was sitting empty and unused. He was very interested in the huge barns. They were full of old farm equipment and tools. Plus the farm had an excellent creek to fish in and the barns were full of fishing equipment left over from its heyday as a popular resort. Local farmers would use it from time to time to pasture their cows or plant a few extra acres of wheat or corn.

Lately JT had noticed strange tire tracks in the driveway as he entered the property. They were fresh tracks because the grass was flat against the ground and the treads were deep and clear because the ground had been wet after recent rains.

JT wandered around the barns and looked for any signs of recent activity. He felt a special attachment and concern for the old place. He had listened attentively whenever friends of his father spoke of the owner and his attempt to run a modern dairy operation. He loved the story Joseph told of how brave his father was that day the infamous bull came to town. John was a hero to his youngest son. He had seen him bravely stand up to the leader of the Klansmen that night many years ago.

Someone had been in the barn and it appeared that a car had parked there. Fresh oil puddled on the floor and had been spread by a tire recently. The tire markings lead from the center of the horse barn back outside before disappearing into the grass and dirt.

John went home that day but he was determined to keep an eye on the Clough farm and see if he could find out what was going on. He decided he would take his fishing pole the next day. On the way down to the creek he would check the place out again. If anyone was hanging around there he would appear to be just an innocent kid going fishing.

The next day after school, instead of taking the lower road home, JT continued down the dirt road until he came to the old farm. A few cows grazed in the pasture as a warm breeze gently blew the overgrown wheat. As he continued through the field the bees buzzed around the clover and grasshoppers jumped in front of his feet as he walked slowly toward the huge horse barn.

He kept looking around him as he walked, not expecting to see anything unusual but just being cautious. There weren't any cars or anything in the barn. Not even a horse was in the stalls. Mr. Troyer often kept a few horses in the barn during the winter months but now they were grazing in the pasture up the road.

As he entered the barn the birds that were nesting near the doorway flew off in a flurry of wings right over his head. That movement startled him for a brief moment and he chuckled to himself for being so jumpy.

He continued walking through the barn toward a small horse cart sitting in the middle of the cement floor. A rat scurried out from under the wheel as he drew closer to the cart. At one time the cart had been used to transfer hay from one stall to another. A pitchfork still stood beside the cart as if inviting him to stop playing around and get to work.

There wasn't a sound in the huge barn. JT looked inside the cart but all he saw was a little straw and a lot of dust and dirt that had probably been there for years.

JT knew there was a basement under the barn. He had been in it just once when he was with his father and the then caretaker of the property. The caretaker wanted John to see the secret room under the barn where the wealthy men came to drink and gamble years ago. The hidden room underneath the barn was the perfect spot for the den of iniquity. The cement walls muffled any noise and no one knew it existed, outside the men who once were the well-to- do guests of Mr. Clough himself.

JT wasn't sure he remembered just how to gain access to the "lift" that operated from the ground floor to the basement. He was just along as a little kid that day and no one paid any attention to his presence. He wandered around the tack room. He did remember being in that room. The smell of the saddles and harnesses brought back a lot of memories. He had been very impressed by the many saddles and pieces of tack needed for all the horses on the farm.

He was rubbing his hand over a particularly large saddle when he espied a saddle blanket that had been dislodged and was lying on the floor. He walked over to pick it up and at that moment he remembered the caretaker doing the exact same thing before grabbing a handle and swinging it forward away from the wall.

JT grabbed the handle and pulled it toward him. In doing so, a door miraculously appeared on the other side of the wall. JT opened the door and there was the lift he remembered as a toddler.

He didn't want to make any noise so he hesitated and looked around to see if there was any sign someone might be down below. He closed the door and stood quietly for a few minutes listening as hard as he could. He noticed a hook jutting out from the wall across the room. It had a saddle blanket and some reins hanging from its curve.

JT crossed the floor quietly. He was getting a little nervous but he knew he just had to find out if anything was going on under the barn. When he pulled the hook a door slid open and there was a stairway leading down to the basement. He held his breath and took the first step down praying it wouldn't creak and give his presence away. At the same time he pulled the door behind him so it would close but not all the way. He wouldn't want to be stuck in the basement with no way out! He might need an escape route pretty darn quick if he got himself in trouble.

Slowly he descended the stairs until they ended near a small hallway. It was very dark. He wished he had brought a few matches. He could just barely make out a door that had some light shining underneath it as he crept along holding on to the wall.

He stopped and listened at the door. Very slowly he eased the door open, expecting any second for someone on the other side to grab it and throw it open and pull him into who knows what. Why was he doing this? He was getting cold feet and was about to turn and run back up the stairs when he thought he heard someone singing. It sounded like a little kid. Mystified he pushed the door open a little further. He could just make out a small form huddled on the floor next to a lantern.

Looking around he didn't see anything else in the room so he cautiously entered a little further and made his way over to the child who was singing in a chant-like voice. As he drew closer he could see it was a little girl. She was in a fetal position and had a blanket drawn up around her and was holding tightly to a small doll. Her eyes were closed and she seemed almost asleep.

Not wanting to scare her to death, JT touched her very gently and whispered softly in her ear.

"Don't be afraid little girl. My name is John Tanner and I'm here to help you so don't cry out or make a sound, okay?"

At the sound of his voice the little girl jumped but she didn't cry out. She slowly turned and looked at him and without uttering a word she threw her arms around his neck and clung to him like she never wanted to let go.

JT wasn't taking any chances that someone would come at any minute and discover them, so he carried her to the stairs and went back up them as quickly as he could. He was big for his age but he was still just a boy and the little girl looked to be about five or six. He tried to put her down but she refused to let go of his neck so he struggled up the steps until he reached the top and almost dropped her on the floor, his arms were so tired.

"Listen, little girl" he began as he hurriedly looked around the barn. "We have to get out of here before anyone comes and finds us. You have to promise to be very quiet and follow me because I can't carry you any more. Do you understand?"

The little girl just nodded and reached for his hand. Together they ran to the side of the entrance to the barn and JT peeked around the open door. Convinced no one was nearby he grabbed her hand and took off running for the creek as fast as he could go. Surprisingly his charge kept up with him until they both collapsed on the bank, their breath coming hard as they gasped for air.

"I'm hungry" the little girl cried, putting her thumb in her mouth and whimpering slightly.

"We'll get you something to eat as soon as I can get you to my house. What's your name anyway?"

"My real name's Moira but everyone calls me Mori." The little girl looked around her and began to cry.

"Now don't cry Mori. I promise I'll take care of you. My mom will know just what to do." John Tanner sure hoped she would because he didn't know what to do with this little girl who was crying and hungry. He hadn't planned on finding a little girl when he went into the barn! He had no idea what was going on but he knew his parents would get to the bottom of it. The problem was getting her from here to there. It was a long walk but they had no choice.

"What were you doing in the barn, Mori? Where do you live?" John asked her as he began to lead her away from the creek.

"I live in Pittsburgh on Staten Drive" she stated clearly as if reciting something she had been taught in school. "I was walking home from school when these bad men grabbed me and threw me into a car. They covered my head with a blanket and when I woke up I was in this place. My gramma and grampa are going to be so mad at them! I was so scared and I cried and begged them to take me home but they just told me to be quiet." She began crying again and soon she started to hiccup.

"Listen Mori," John said as he helped her up climb up the bank. "This is my plan. We'll cross the pasture over there and then cross the road and go up through the woods until we come to my house. You will have to stay close to me and not make any noise. Do you think you can do that?"

Seeing her nod JT took her hand and started across the pasture. He darted between several cows as they sidestepped cowpies, finally making it to the side of the road. Not seeing any cars or wagons coming, JT pulled her across the road and up over a ditch and on into the woods. Once they were under the cover of the trees JT felt a lot more secure.

They stopped to rest several times as it was a tough climb up the hill but JT wanted to stay in the woods and not risk being seen on the open road. When he finally spotted the back of the barn he breathed a sigh of relief as they came out of the woods into the yard.

Katie happened to be coming out of the chicken coop when she saw her son and a strange little girl walking toward her looking disheveled and frightened.

"John Tanner Wjotla where have you been?" demanded Katie as she walked toward him carrying a basket of eggs. "You should have been home from school hours ago!"

Before John Tanner could respond, Katie had forgotten all about him and was kneeling down by Mori.

"Who is this darling wee child, John Tanner, and why is she so dirty and looking so frightened?" Katie took the little girl's hand and began walking toward the house.

JT began to open his mouth to explain but thought better of it. He continued across the yard and into the back door of the house. As soon as he sat down Mori ran over and slid into the chair with him as if she was afraid to ever leave his side.

"Don't be scared, Mori," he explained. "My mom will understand everything as soon as we tell her your story. She will help you find your grandparents, I promise."

That made the little girl feel better but she still refused to leave her rescuer's side.

The last thing John Tanner wanted was for her to begin crying again and get him into even more trouble.

Katie put down the basket of eggs and went back out to get the load of laundry she had just removed from the line. She needed a few minutes to compose herself and let the little girl feel comfortable in her home. She didn't know what had happened but she could see how frightened she was and how much she wanted to be with John Tanner.

When Katie came back into the kitchen she saw both of the children sitting in the same chair, the little girl pressed up tight against her son with her little face awash with tears. Her heart just broke at the sight of her son trying to be so brave yet a look of total bewilderment was on his face. She went over and knelt down by the chair and slowly drew the little girl into her arms.

"There, there little one. What has happened to cause these tears?

Has John Tanner hurt you in any way?" she inquired, at the same time giving her son a threatening look.

"N-n-no ma'am," Mori stammered, not wanting to cry but finding it hard to stop the flow of tears. She felt safe in this woman's arms and wanted to hide in them forever.

"Mama," began JT, "I found Mori in the basement under the barn at the old Clough farm. She lives in Pittsburgh but was kidnapped by the KKK and brought here. I found her there and brought her home so you could help her!" JT couldn't get the words out of his mouth fast enough as his eyes implored his mother to believe him and do something, anything to get him off the hook.

"What?" exclaimed Katie, finding it hard to believe what her son had just said. "Tell me the story again John Tanner, just a little bit slower, please."

JT related the whole story again, including how he knew about the room under the barn and what drew him to be there in the first place.

Katie sat and listened, holding the wee girl in her arms and patting her back and stroking her hair. She was astonished but very proud of what her son had done. Sometimes he was so mature she was surprised to discover he was the same boy who just yesterday had been admonished for putting a skunk in the outhouse.

John was at work and they didn't have a phone so she did the next best thing and sent John Tanner down the road to a neighbor's house so the police could be contacted.

The three of them were in the kitchen having some cookies and milk when the police drove into the driveway. John just happened to pull in right after them so the whole story had to be repeated again.

Mori was sound asleep by the time the authorities had finished

81

questioning her. Katie had given her a bath and put her in one of the twin's old nighties. They decided it would be best for her to stay the night with the Wjotla family until her grandparents could be notified and dispatched to pick her up.

Once it was determined this was the child who had been kidnapped, events began to happen quickly. John Tanner was angry all over again when he found out the Ku Klux Klan was behind the kidnapping. He demanded the police do something to find these cowards and put them behind bars forever! What if he hadn't found her? What if she had died down in the basement of the barn? There she was, a little girl, all alone in a strange place.

Katie and John attempted to calm down their youngest child who was so upset over this incident. They tried to tell him it was over now and Mori was safe because of his brave actions. Her grandparents would come and take her home and everything would be alright.

One of the deputies remained at the farm for the night and the others left to begin the process of contacting the grandparents and set the legal process into motion.

It was a long night in the Wjotla household. John and Katie had a difficult time getting to sleep. John Tanner insisted on sleeping on the floor next to the bed where Mori slept. He felt an obligation to see her safely through until her grandparents came. Every sound caused him to spring awake and he would jump up and check to see she was okay.

JT refused to go to school the next day. He wanted to be there when Mori's grandparents came to get her. When the long black car finally pulled into the driveway, Mori squealed with glee and ran out into the yard to welcome her grandparents. The judge grabbed her right up in a big hug and twirled her around before handing her over to her grandmother. She threw her arms around her grandmother's neck and held on like she never wanted to let go.

"So where is this young man who rescued my granddaughter?" the judge demanded as he entered the house, his deep voice booming and filling the room with his presence.

"Poppa, here he is, this is John Tanner!" Mori cried as she pulled JT into the room.

Looking a bit sheepish and embarrassed at all the attention, JT looked up at this impressive man in all his finery. He offered his hand to the judge and found himself enveloped in a bear hug and slapped on the back until he thought he would surely be crushed.

"Thank you, thank you, young man" the judge and his wife said again and again. "You have no idea how worried we were about our little Mori. We are so relieved and thankful she is okay."

Once again the whole story had to be retold. This time Mori sat on her grandfather's lap with her arm around his shoulders. You could tell that they were very close and she loved her grandparents very much.

Soon it was time to say goodbye. Many thanks were exchanged once again. Mori hugged JT and promised to write to him as soon as she learned how to write. Addresses were exchanged and Judge Quinn left an open invitation to have the Wjotla family visit them anytime they were in Pittsburgh. He drew JT aside and made a promise to him that anything he could ever do for him, he was just a phone call away.

The incident was on the front page of all the area newspapers for a few days but soon it became just back page news. John Tanner read the paper religiously for weeks but never saw where the perpetrators were caught or convicted of any crime. He knew it had to be local KKK members because no one else knew of the secret room. Someone who lived close by had to be responsible for feeding her and taking her water.

The Ku Klux Klan disappeared from the area after the little girl was found. The public was incensed over the incident and the Klan knew they had overstepped the boundaries. There was talk of running the known Klan members out of town on a rail. Eventually the talk simmered down and things returned to normal.

The kidnapping and rescue were never forgotten but it soon became set aside as talk of war began to filter in from across the sea.

CHAPTER ELEVEN

WHEN FRANKLIN D. Roosevelt was elected President, he introduced the "New Deal" reforms which gave the government more power and helped ease the Depression. Other nations were also changing their leaders and their type of government.

In Germany, poor economic conditions led to the rise of power of the dictator, Adolf Hitler. The Japanese invaded China, developing industries and mines in Manchuria. The Japanese claimed this growth would relieve the Depression. This militarism of the Germans and Japanese eventually led to World War II.

The attack on Pearl Harbor on December 7, 1941, was like an arrow had been struck straight through the heart of most Americans. Men and boys clambered into any vehicle nearby and made their way to the recruiting offices. Joseph and James Wjotla were no exception. They left their jobs and joined the army that very first week after the President declared war on Japan.

John Tanner begged to go with his brothers but his parents talked him into staying in school and helping out on the home front. Reluctantly he finally agreed but he wasn't happy about seeing his brothers' leave without him.

Joseph and James both joined the Army but they were sent to different bases for basic training. They wrote home regularly so everyone would know where they were and how they were doing. JT ran to the mailbox every day looking for letters from his brothers. If there was a letter in the mailbox he would race in the house and hand it to his mother and everyone would sit around the table while she opened and read it aloud.

By the early 1940's Marjorie and Irene were the only girls still living at home. They both had boyfriends and jobs and were looking forward to getting engaged.

Maria and Martina had moved to Washington, D.C. They both found jobs working in government offices. They shared an apartment in the city and were happy to be independent. The declaration of war brought new excitement to the capital city and they often wrote home describing the people they met and the places they had been.

John was no longer working at the factory. A new Polish Club had been built in town and he was managing it. Katie did the cooking while he ran the bar and kept up the grounds. They had a small apartment above the club and lived there during the week after John Tanner began high school.

Their neighbors milked the cows and fed all the livestock during the week. The twins tended the garden, fed the chickens and gathered the eggs. They took care of the house and made sure everything was neat and tidy before they left for work in the morning. They saved their money and bought a car. Marjorie worked in the office at Aero Supply. It was a manufacturing plant that manufactured things for the military. Irene did bookkeeping at Raymond Spring Corporation. One would drop the other off and then go on to her job. They would assign a place to meet after work and then drive home together. Sometimes they would join their parents and brother for dinner at the club.

Marjorie's boyfriend had joined the Navy and was serving on a ship in the South Pacific. When he left she was sure she would never see him again. Marjorie had never been out of Pennsylvania, so to her the South Pacific was like being on another planet.

Irene's boyfriend was an aviator and he was stationed at a base in Alaska. He liked it there but often wrote that it was very remote and if it weren't for his buddies he would be very homesick.

The community as a whole was very supportive of their boys overseas and the families at home. The newspaper welcomed stories from the soldiers and printed pictures and letters daily.

John Tanner continued to receive letters from his friend Mori Quinn in Pittsburgh. Her grandfather was running for Congress. Mori was excited about moving to Washington D.C. She wanted to go to the Washington Zoo and take a tour of all the monuments. JT answered her letters. He asked her how she was doing in school and what her activities were. He loved getting her letters. He felt he was her guardian angel. He felt strongly about looking out for her best interests for the rest of her life..

JT played football for his high school team. He was the top player in the district. He was a very good student and was voted President of his class. His gregariousness made him popular and one of the most well liked boys in the high school.

He missed his brothers. He eagerly awaited any word regarding the war. He became the first one the other families contacted when they received a letter from their sons and daughters who were in the conflict. They knew how closely he followed the war and how interested he was about the welfare of every soldier whether he knew them personally or not.

The Polish Club was doing very well. It was a place the townspeople could gather and have a good meal and drink and play cards or just sit and chat with one another. The citizens of Polish descent could always find one or two recent Polish newspapers. John and Katie had them mailed from Chicago.

Katie enjoyed the change of pace of the club from the loneliness of the farm. She and John had many friends in the community. They were well-liked and much respected.

JT helped out at the club but he also worked on weekends at Wing Willie's. Wing Willies was a grocery store right smack dab in the middle of downtown. JT stocked the shelves and made the deliveries. He enjoyed seeing all the customers. Everyone remarked at what a fine boy he was. They followed his football career religiously. Everyone in town was hoping for an undefeated season that year.

JT went to work hoping he would get a chance to see Mary Ellen Watkins. He went to school with Mary Ellen, although he was in a class ahead of her. She was a tall girl who played on the basketball team. She had the most beautiful brown hair and the bluest eyes he had ever seen. He was smitten by her smile.

On Saturdays Mary Ellen would come into the store with her mother. Mrs. Watkins was kind of snooty, he thought. She was the wife of the town's attorney so he surmised she had to have certain airs about her. He didn't care what she thought about him. He just wanted to feast his eyes on Mary Ellen and dream about getting enough nerve to ask her out on a date.

Mary Ellen liked JT too but she was shy and couldn't speak to him without stammering all over the place like a nitwit. One day when she was reaching for an item on an upper shelf for her mother, JT came running over and reached up to get it down for her. Their fingers actually touched reaching for the item at the same time.! She was certain electricity had just struck the store and she was about to die.

JT almost dropped the can of peas right in the middle of the store. All at once it seemed as if they were the only two people in the universe as they stared into each other's eyes.

"Ahem", Mrs. Watkins said, looking at her daughter with reproach. "I think I have what I need for now, Mary Ellen. Let's pay for these items and go pick up your father at his office."

With that, JT was dismissed and his newfound love disappeared out the door in a flurry of petticoats.

It wasn't long after that episode that JT got the nerve to invite Mary Ellen to a school dance. She wasn't allowed to ride in a car with him alone. He assured her his sisters would drive them and pick them up and deliver her home. This satisfied her parent's so on the night in question he showed up at her door in his best slacks and sweater.

His sisters let them off a few blocks from the high school and continued on their way to meet their friends. John told them they would walk home with other friends so he could spend more time with Mary Ellen.

They stopped at the Fountainette to have a soda but he made sure he had her home by the required time. He politely said goodnight and walked away, all the time hoping he could just grab her and kiss the daylights out of those sweet red lips!

Irene and Marjorie got a kick out of taking their brother and Mary Ellen to the movies and dances. They let Mary Ellen borrow their lipstick and rouge and laughed when she tried to wipe it all off before she got back home. They knew how strict her parents were and they made sure she never missed a curfew.

Mary Ellen thought John Tanner was the cutest boy in school. He was certainly the smartest and the best athlete. All the other girls flirted with him and even invited him to their houses for dinner. JT only had eyes for Mary Ellen. His friends teased him unmercifully but he didn't care. He just kept smiling to himself and thinking only about her and the next time they would be together.

JT worked on the farm during the summer months. The hard

work kept him in shape for football. He not only worked his family's farm but he put in hay for several neighboring farms. Once in awhile Mary Ellen would drive out with her friends to say hello. There he'd be in the hayfield with his shirt off looking all tanned and sweaty and her heart would just thump in her chest. She hadn't experienced anything but a few kisses and an occasional brush of his fingers across her breast, but something was definitely stirring her insides.

John and Katie had raised their children to be respectful of their bodies and always responsible for their actions. Sex was never openly discussed but when you're raised on a farm it isn't long before you know about the birds and the bees.

JT had the same stirrings in his body and was more than eager to explore these new feelings. He wished Mary Ellen wouldn't look at him like she wanted to devour him piece by piece. It was very unsettling and he fairly threw the hay bales into the wagon just to battle the way he was feeling and what his body displayed. Lord, he prayed….just get back in the car and leave!

JT had his heart set on going to the United States Military Academy after high school. He wanted to be a soldier like his brothers but he wanted even more. He was determined to become an officer and maybe later go into politics. Like all ambitious young people he wanted to change the world!

His counselor had told him he had to be recommended by a State Senator or Congressman or even the President himself! John Tanner finally sat down and wrote a letter to Judge Quinn explaining his plans for the future. He asked the Judge to put a good word in for him if he became elected the Senator from Pennsylvania. To his surprise he received a letter back saying the Judge would be honored to make the required recommendation on his behalf. Judge Michael Riley Quinn thought a great deal of John Tanner

Wjotla. He and his wife, Genevieve, thought the sun rose and set on their granddaughter, Moira. They might not have her with them if it hadn't been for the young man from the small town in northwest Pennsylvania. They would do anything for him.

CHAPTER TWELVE

IN THE fall the family received a letter from Maria. She was engaged. She and her fiancé, Captain Grant MacGregor, would be coming home for Christmas so he could meet her family. Maria and Grant had met at a party in Washington. Maria worked for the Navy Department and her boss had invited her to a dinner party he was hosting for some military officers who were in Washington for a few days on leave from their ship. Captain MacGregor had been one of the officers. Maria had fallen head over heels for the young officer. Before he left the city he had promised to write her every day. They corresponded on a regular basis. Before he returned to port he sent a telegram asking if she would marry him.

Katie was thrilled to be planning a wedding for her oldest daughter. The wedding would be at the Saint Thomas Catholic Church but the reception would be held at the Polish Club. Katie would make certain it was the wedding of the year!

John and JT drove to the train station in Erie to pick Maria and Captain MacGregor up a few days before Christmas. The captain just had a week's leave so it would be a quick turnaround. The family was grateful they had the opportunity to meet him and see Maria again. It had been a few years since they had seen their daughter and sister.

The train station was bustling. People were laughing and embracing. The joy of the holiday was everywhere. John couldn't help but remember the train station in New York City all those years ago. Now here he was, old enough to be a grandfather with grown sons off in Europe fighting a war. Where had the time gone?

Military uniforms were everywhere, all branches of the service, both officers and enlisted men. The soldiers got off the train and searched the crowd for a loved one. Many couples were embracing. Women were crying and children were running around the platform. It was quite chaotic but wonderful at the same time.

JT spotted Maria first and gave a shout. He grabbed his father by the coat sleeve and dragged him over to the train steps.

Maria flew into her brother's outstretched arms. She hugged her father and they all began talking at once.

They laughed at each other when they remembered there was another person in their party. They took a few steps back and waited for her fiancé to make his way down the steps. Captain MacGregor was in full uniform and looked very handsome indeed. Maria clutched his arm and brought him over to meet her father and brother.

"Papa, I would like you to meet my fiancé, Captain Grant MacGregor" she said proudly. John shook the man's outstretched hand and said he was happy to meet him. He then turned to his son and introduced the Captain to JT.

Looking at JT and giving Maria a wink he put his hand on the boy's shoulder and grabbed his hand. "I've been looking forward to meeting you John Tanner. Your sister has told me many stories about her little brother. Are they true or should I disregard them?"

JT laughed and immediately replied. "That might surely be the case, Captain, but I would like to have a turn telling you some stories about Maria!"

"John Tanner, don't you dare do any such thing!" Maria cried as they all laughed. The men collected the baggage and walked to the parking lot.

A light snow began to fall as they neared Corry. Captain MacGregor was captivated by it. He was from southern Arizona and hadn't experienced much snow. John assured him he would probably see a lot more before his visit was over.

Katie met them at the door. She was happy they made it home before the snowfall became any heavier. She liked Maria's young man instantly. She decided he was the perfect mate for Maria. Grant shared a room with JT. They soon became fast friends. JT took him to the barn to help with the chores and the Captain grabbed a pitchfork and dug right in. He told JT he was raised on his parent's ranch so he knew a thing or too about pitching hay.

Martina didn't make it home that year for Christmas but she promised to be there for the wedding. The family received letters from Joseph and James. Joseph was still somewhere in Europe but James had been reassigned to the Philippines. John and Katie had no idea where that country was located. Grant found a map and drew a line from Pennsylvania to the islands so they would know exactly where their son was.

Irene's boyfriend was also home on leave so she spent most of the time at his family's home. Marjorie hadn't heard from her friend Sam in a few months so she was kind of down in the dumps over the holidays. The family made a special effort to bring her into the celebration. Soon she was gaily sledding or ice skating with everyone else.

Katie and John felt they were blessed to be sharing this Christmas with so many of their children. Many families were left with just memories that year. Their loved ones would never be joining them again. They counted their blessings and prayed for all the soldiers who were without family that holiday.

Maria and Grant left for Washington the day after Christmas. Grant was being deployed to England and wanted to spend some time with his family before shipping out. His parents and younger sister were coming to Washington to see him off. They would be meeting Maria for the first time. Maria was looking forward to meeting her future in-laws and also Grant's little sister. Wedding plans could definitely be made now that both sets of parents had been informed and introduced to the prospective bride and groom.

Katie and John celebrated the New Year with their friends and families at the Polish Club. JT brought Mary Ellen and also encouraged her parents to join in the celebration. Mr. and Mrs. Watkins actually danced the polka and joined in singing and toasting the new year along with all the other party goers.

JT and Mary Ellen grabbed a couple of cokes and went out to his parent's car to toast the New Year in private. JT gave her his class ring and asked her to be his girl. When she whispered yes they embraced and kissed. Soon they were necking and taking off their coats and kissing again. JT had his hand under her sweater and had made his way to her breast when suddenly the fireworks went off and startled them both back into reality. Flushed, they hurriedly put their coats back on and ran back into the club grinning and holding hands.

Many resolutions and promises were made that night that didn't come to fruition. That was part of life. Luckily the prayers of many were answered when the Armistice was signed months later and the war came to an end.

Katie spent many hours planning Maria's wedding. She was hoping Joseph and James would be home before the wedding day. Joseph wrote to say he had fallen in love with an English girl and was getting married. The news was met with joy and expectation.

Katie couldn't wait to meet the new bride. Joseph was her quiet son. She had a feeling this wife he had chosen would make a huge difference in his life. Her family was changing daily.

CHAPTER THIRTEEN

J OSEPH DIDN'T make it home in time for the wedding. James arrived a few days before. He had contacted malaria and was very gaunt and undernourished. Katie vowed to fatten him up. Everyone was happy to have him home. He was very quiet and withdrawn. The family thought it would just take some time. They hoped that soon he would be their own James. He was overwhelmed by the changes around the farm. He was surprised his parents were so happy to be living in town and running the Polish Club. James had always been a farm boy. He told them he wanted to stay home and run the farming operation

Captain MacGregor and Maria arrived a few days before the wedding. They had to rush to get everything ready because Grant had to leave right after the wedding. He had been re-assigned to Hawaii. They were very excited about beginning their life together as a married couple and moving to a new place.

Grant's sister, Susan, was in the wedding party. She and her parents arrived the day before the wedding. There wasn't room for them at the farm so Katie and John let them have their rooms at the Polish Club. This worked out fine because that was where the reception was being held. They were there to help decorate.

John liked Grant's father. He was a rancher and they could discuss farming techniques and horses. Dan MacGregor was an avid horseman. His herd numbered well over two hundred at his spread in Arizona. He invited John and Katie down to the ranch to be their guests. John said he would certainly look forward to that!

Martina was home for the wedding just like she had promised. She brought with her a wispy little man whom she introduced as Dr. Arthur Matthews. He was at least twenty years her senior. They seemed to be very much in love and doted on each other all the time they were there. The family welcomed him but gave her strange looks when she wasn't looking.

JT thought it was amusing to see the family's reaction. He took every opportunity to get Arthur to help with the chores. The doctor was a good sport about it and it wasn't long before JT thought he was a good guy after all. He told Martina Arthur was a great match for her.

Irene's boyfriend never returned from the war. She didn't waste time fretting and stewing about her loss. She moved on with her life. It wasn't long before she found someone new where she worked. His name was Franklin McCray. Generations of his family had been living in Corry for well over one hundred years. Irene was one of the bridesmaids at her sister's wedding. She spent the whole time at the altar giggling and looking at Franklin.

Marjorie was also a bridesmaid. Her boyfriend was coming home in a few weeks. He planned to return to San Diego to live and wanted her to go back with him. He was going to go to school on the GI Bill and work in the shipyards at night. Marjorie planned on getting a job as a secretary as soon as they settled. She told her mother they were getting married as soon as Fred arrived. It would be a small wedding with just immediate family members present. Katie assured her that would be okay. She tried to find the time to help her get things together. It was a very busy time.

The wedding went off without a hitch and before you knew it, both Marjorie and Maria were married and gone. The house seemed empty. Martina had gone back to Washington with Arthur and Irene found an apartment in town.

Joseph and his bride, Margaret, arrived at the farm in late August. She had the brightest red hair the family had ever seen. They fell in love with her immediately and went out of their way to make her feel welcome. She loved America and was quick to adjust and accept the changes in her life.

Joseph bought the property next to the farm. He went to work at a local factory in town, just like his dad had done years ago.

Margaret adored Katie and John. She spent a lot of time with Katie. They shopped together and Katie introduced her at church. Margaret joined the quilting club and before you knew it, she felt right at home.

CHAPTER FOURTEEN

I N THE fall of that year, JT was a senior in high school. He was President of the senior class and was Co-Captain of the varsity football team. He was an altar boy at Saint Thomas Church and was named Rotary Club Boy of the Year.

Judge Quinn, now Senator Quinn, came through with the appointment to the United States Military Academy for John Tanner Wjotla. News of the appointment appeared in the local newspaper and also the Erie Times. You would have thought Mary Ellen's father was the parent as he strutted around town spreading the news.

Katie and John were so proud of their son. John broke down and cried when he read the letter from West Point. He and Katie clung to each other as they read and re-read the wonderful news.

JT was very excited when he received the letter and couldn't wait to tell Mary Ellen of his appointment. He was disappointed when she didn't respond quite the way he had hoped. In fact, she seemed downright depressed.

"What's the matter, Mary Ellen? This is the best news of my life! You act like you don't even care!" John was getting angry and began walking away.

"Wait, JT," she cried out as she ran up to him and put her hand on his arm. She paused a moment to blow her nose into her hankie.

"I am happy for you, JT, I really am. You have wanted this for so long. I'm just upset because this means you'll be going away and I won't see you for a very long time."

"Oh, Mary Ellen, it won't be that bad, I promise" JT assured her as he put his arm around her and tried to think of something comforting to say. "Let's just forget about this for now and go see a movie or something. Okay?"

"Okay," sniffed Mary Ellen and she began to break into a little smile. "It's a long time off anyway JT. Maybe you will even change your mind before next summer."

JT pretended not to hear that statement as he patted her hand and helped her into his car and drove to the movie theater. He would leave today for West Point if he could. It had been his dream forever and nothing would keep him from going, not even Mary Ellen Watkins!

School was an exciting place to be that fall. Being a senior was the best. The seniors ruled the school. They ran all the activities and received special treatment from the teachers. Pep rallies were held every Thursday night before the big game.

Homecoming was just a day away. The team would be playing their biggest game of the season. It was also Parents night and JT was looking forward to walking out on the field with Katie and John. His parents were the greatest as far as he was concerned.

JT was going to the pep rally with other members of the football team. They all wore their letter sweaters and jeans. After the rally they would grab their dates and head for the Fountainette to have a pizza or grab a burger.

It was a lovely fall evening. The air was crisp and just a hint of a breeze was blowing. Many residents of Corry were burning leaves in their yards. Kids were running around enjoying the last chance to be out in the evening air before the snow began falling. They would be forced to stay inside during the long winter nights.

North of downtown Corry were the Corry Fairgrounds. The

Fairgrounds included a horse racing track which was the main attraction on summer nights in the small town. Quarter horses were raised and trained in the area and brought to the fairgrounds to race. It was a big draw for residents of Northwestern Pennsylvania. Entire families came and spent the day with their picnic baskets in tow with jackets put aside for later when the night became chilly.

Tonight was the final race of the season. Labor Day was usually the last race but the good weather had enticed the owners of the horses to stick around and race a few more weekends.

A lot of families had built bonfires and were roasting hot dogs and marshmallows while waiting for the rest of the crowd to arrive. John and Katie had been talked into coming by friends who had stopped by the club on their way to the last race of the year. John at first declined but soon he gave in to their good natured pressure. They gathered their jackets and blankets and left with the couple for the track.

"Wow" remarked John as they neared the fairgrounds "there's a big crowd tonight. I hope we can find a parking place."

"Look at all the bonfires" exclaimed Katie as she gathered their things from the trunk of the car.

"I hope everyone is careful," their friend Walter remarked as they walked together toward the grandstand. "I see sparks blowing around all over the place!"

John looked at the wooden grandstands and back at the bonfires burning close by. "That could be a problem if the wind picks up," he surmised, glancing over at the wooden barns and stables. He shook his head and urged his wife along toward the seating area. "I guess some people just don't have any common sense these days."

The races soon began and before you knew it, the horses were lining up for the last race. The wind had really picked up. The night was growing colder so Katie put her coat on. She was reaching for her scarf when a gust of wind snatched it up and away it flew, sailing behind the grandstand.

She started to get up and go after it when John drew her gently down to her seat. He told her to sit still, he would get her scarf.

She held on to his hand for a brief moment and thanked him for being so gallant. He just smiled at her, gave her a wink and then he was gone.

John had just vacated the grandstand when the cry of "Fire! Fire!" rang out from the crowd. Everyone's attention was drawn to the barn nearest the parking area. Flames were spewing from the roof. The crowd could hear the whinnying and frightened screams from the horses inside the barn.

"Call the fire department" someone yelled. "Hurry!"

"Someone bring a hose and some buckets!" another voice cried.

The crowd began to run from the grandstand, dragging blankets and sacks of food, grabbing children and running as fast as they could toward their cars in the field beyond.

"Come on Katie!" shouted her friend Bess as they clambered down the rickety steps of the grandstand.

"Where's John?" Katie cried looking under the bleachers and not seeing his plaid shirt. "I don't see him anywhere, Bess!"

"Don't worry about John, Katie! Walter will find him. They are probably already on the way over to help the fire department. Come on! We'll wait for them back at the club. Let's get out of here before the fire trucks get here and block the exit. It's getting colder and we don't want to be stuck here!"

Bess was one of the few women Katie knew who drove a car. Katie was learning but so far John did all the driving. At the moment they didn't care who did or didn't drive. The two women just wanted to be away from the sight of the fire and all the crazy people running all over frightened and out of control.

Most of the men ran to help put out the fires. The fire was spreading to other barns nearby. Many of the men were leading the horses from the nearby stables and letting them loose to fend for themselves.

Katie didn't see Walter or John but she knew they would be there right in the thick of things. That's just the way they were. She finally gave up looking for them and let herself be led away to the car. It took them a long time to make it out to the street but they finally got out on the main road and made their way back to the club to wait it out.

JT was just parking his car behind the Fountainette when a car came to a screeching stop and shouted out the window that the racetrack was on fire and the firemen needed all the help they could get.

JT got back into his car and drove Mary Ellen home before going on to the fairgrounds. The place was a whirlwind of activity. He had to stop and park the car a good half mile from the parking area. He could see the giant flames as they danced their way across the sky.

He ran as fast as he could and began helping a group of men who were dragging equipment out of the second barn. He recognized Walter and asked him where his dad was. Walter said John had gone into the barn to help get the horses out. JT ran to the entrance of the barn but all he could see was smoke and flames. The massive doorway was just filled with hot air and choking black smoke.

JT could barely see inside the barn. He was coughing and his eyes were burning and tearing and he had to back away. He saw a figure running toward him, each hand holding the bridle of a horse frightened out of its mind and trying to rear up and thrash out with its hooves but the man kept running and tugging them on. As the figure drew closer JT could see it was his father. He attempted to rise and run forward to give him a helping hand. He was forcefully pulled back by hands that pushed him back to the ground.

He glanced up just in time to see the beam holding up the doorway give way and begin falling toward the ground. He screamed for his father to release the horses and just run!

"Leave the horses Papa!" he pleaded. "Run Papa, run!" He was screaming, trying desperately to get to his feet.

Just then the beam gave way completely and came crashing down. The roof collapsed, enveloping the entire barn in flames.

JT and the men around him were stunned into disbelief. It was a few seconds before any of them could respond.

JT was the first one to run forward and scream for his father, pleading with whoever would listen to help him find his dad.

Hands again held him back and he was encircled with arms that slowly drew him away from the flames.

Walter had him in his arms and they were both sobbing, overcome with grief and heartbreak, knowing their friend and father was lying beneath that beam along with the horses he was so desperately trying to save.

Katie knew it too. Her heart was breaking and she cried and cried, even before she got the news. She just knew. Her beloved John was dead and now she was alone. Her life mate who had stood beside her for over thirty years was gone in a flash.

Walter came to the club with John Tanner. One look at her friend and her son confirmed all her fears. Mother and son embraced, sobbing uncontrollably. Their friends stayed the night, holding Katie and JT tightly, talking about John and what a wonderful man he was. It was a heartbreaking experience for all of them.

The children gathered over the next few days and made plans to bury their father. Katie was inconsolable. Neighbors were coming and going all day bringing food and asking what they could do to help.

The church was filled to overflowing the day of the funeral. Everyone from town came to pay their respects to the family of John Wjotla. His children stood by the casket and received the condolences and murmured their thanks.

The funeral service was attended by hundreds of people. Firemen attended en masse. They looked very imposing as they sat together wearing their full uniforms and black arm bands. They had come from towns all over the area to pay their respects to this man who volunteered and gave his life helping them.

When the priest finished his remarks, JT walked up to the altar, above where his father's casket lay in repose. He thanked those who had come and all those who had been supportive of the family.

He spoke clearly and his words were precise and full of emotion.

"My father is a hero. He was a hero many times over. He came to this country with my mother when he was just twenty years old. They both had dreams of raising a family in freedom and without fear. He accomplished those things.

My father died doing what he thought was right. I will live my life doing the same and following the rules he set for me and my brothers and sisters.

John Wjotla was a great man. He honored me by being my father."

Jan Pietr Wjotla was buried in St. Thomas Cemetery on a hill overlooking the valley where he had come to find peace. Katie came often to talk to him. She often walked the eleven miles to his grave. He was her hero, her love, her John.

CHAPTER FIFTEEN

WEST POINT, the United States Military Academy, sits on the banks of the Hudson River, about fifty miles north of New York City. The mission of the Academy is to produce Army officers. The Academy opened its doors in 1802. Many of its graduates were true American icons. Names like Robert E. Lee, Stonewall Jackson, Ulysses S. Grant, George Custer, General "BlackJack" Pershing, Dwight D. Eisenhower, General Omar Bradley, General Douglas MacArthur and General William Westmoreland just to name a few, were all graduates of West Point.

The Academy is all about discipline. Tuition is paid but you owe the Army five years of military duty upon graduation. Academic courses and field training are the required curriculum at West Point. Fail two courses and you're out. Fail the military tasks and you're out.

The Army believes officers have got to be physically, mentally, emotionally and ethically ready when they leave the Academy. The training each cadet receives at West Point totally prepares him for leadership upon graduation.

John Tanner was ready to take on his future as he stepped out of the car upon his arrival at West Point. Plebes spend their first summer at Cadet Basic Training. Beast Barracks is what it's called, where the young men get solderized. Five weeks of pure hell. JT came to West Point with his mother and his brother, James. It was the first trip outside of his hometown. He was full of wonder as they passed through the state of Pennsylvania and into New York State. His eyes were glued to the window the entire trip.

James didn't talk much but he watched his brother through the rear view mirror of the old Chevy as he drove along the highways and through many small towns along the way. James was happy just staying home and running the farm. He elected to drive JT to West Point as a favor to his mother. He had taken the reins of the family farm after his father had died. Katie depended on him to take care of things and he obliged. He came home from the war a changed man. He had seen things no one should have to witness.

Joseph had been in the European Theater. He had fought bravely, helping to secure the coast of Normandy. He had been injured during the conflict and was a recipient of the Purple Heart and other commendations. He was lucky enough to find the love of his life and come back safely and resume his life in the Brokenstraw Valley.

James went through the Bataan death march as a Japanese prisoner of war. He couldn't talk about it, even now. He suffered from malaria because of it and would have to take medication the rest of his life. He didn't have the nightmares so much anymore but in his mind he hadn't healed. Each day was an opportunity to forget and forgive. So far he could do neither.

James was very proud of his youngest brother. John Tanner was a great kid and he was so happy he had received the appointment to the United States Military Academy. James knew he would become a fine officer some day. He always had been a leader and he was also very bright. He would do well away from the farm. It was his turn to shine and James would see to it that he had everything he needed to do just that.

Katie sat in the car thinking about the past eighteen years. They had passed so quickly. John Tanner was the light of her life. She loved all her children equally but John Tanner had given her that extra spark. Maybe it was the manner he was conceived, that wonderful night in the barn when she had been so full of love for his father. It was a turning point in her life. Now John was gone and she missed him terribly. He would be a very proud father today. She must concentrate on that and not tear up when she had to say goodbye to her son.

Reception Day at West Point was a wonderful experience. The families had their first glimpse of what West Point was all about. Highland Falls, New York was enjoying a beautiful day for the beginning of summer.

The new candidates were to assemble at the stadium early that June morning. When JT arrived with his mother and brother, he was greeted by Senator Quinn. Senator Quinn threw an arm around JT's shoulder and said how proud he was to be there today. He offered Katie and James his condolences on the death of John. He remarked he was sorry he was not at the funeral but he hadn't heard about the accident until almost a month later when John Tanner had written Mori.

Speaking of his granddaughter, the older man stepped back and scanned the crowd briefly looking for someone. He walked over to a group of women and came back holding the hand of a lovely young girl. His wife also accompanied them and greeted the family warmly. Mrs. Quinn congratulated JT on his appointment and told his mother she would be keeping an eye on this young man! She was sure he would be going places someday. John Tanner could not believe this was the same little Mori Quinn he had last seen six years ago. She was now twelve years old and in junior high school. She threw her arms around him anyway and said she was just thrilled to see him again. Everyone was chatting and enjoying each other's company when a cadet announced the families would have to depart and the candidates would line up to begin their first day at West Point.

John Tanner was a bit nervous. He was ready for this new step but at the same time he was worried about leaving his mother. The past year had been hard for her but he knew she wanted him to succeed and so he took comfort from that.

Everyone said their goodbyes and wished him luck. Mori called out to him to remember to write to her. He waved and went over to assemble with the rest of the guys awaiting their next order.

The next twelve hours would be busy with being divided, weighed, processed and sworn in. The candidates would be tested by upperclassmen wearing red sashes and trained. By sundown a thousand or more former civilians marched smartly across the Plain as uniformed soldiers. Upon completion of Beast Barracks they will be called Plebes. Right now they were officially cadets. All the candidates signed an oath agreeing to protect the Constitution and be loyal to the United States and its sovereignty. That you will serve and defend your country and you agree to follow your officers. They were informed of the Uniform Code of Military Justice which applied to them in and out of uniform, on or off duty, anywhere in the world.

Then came the haircut. Following that experience, all the young men looked alike. Same clothing, same haircut, same frightened look. All the cadets had to line up and at that moment came the first part of their training. They were taught to salute and refer to themselves as "New Cadet____."

When JT fell into his bed that first night he was totally exhausted but excited about this new life. He was in a new place and anxious to take each day as it came. He didn't mind the harassment from the upperclassmen.

The next few weeks went by in a blur. Cadets are required to memorize pages of regulations, attack strategies, terrain, weapons, mottos and traditions. They also master greetings: within days they have to know the names of 125 cadets in his company, hard to do when all 4,000 cadets on post are dressed and barbered the same.

Cadets wake up every morning at 6:30. Plebes are required to stand at attention in the hallway and call out the uniform of the day. At 6:55 they line up outside Washington Hall for ten minutes at Parade Rest for ten minutes. The weather doesn't matter. They are required to do this in rain, sleet, snow, hail or heat. Once a week there is a haircut inspection. Upperclassmen walk the ranks inspecting their uniform, shoes, hair, etc.

Breakfast and lunch, which are mandatory, are eaten at designated tables. Plebes serve the meals. The classes leave in order of rank.

From 0730 to 1600 there are academic classes. After four when the cadets are not at parade drill they are required to participate in athletics. John Tanner played on the football team, so that activity tired him to the point of exhaustion by the time the day was done. They studied at least three hours a night and rarely got more than five hours of sleep before a whole new day began again.

JT's company took the flag for best in the beast. The six weeks was a killer for sure but he made it through and became a Plebe. He was used to being bossed around by older brothers and thrown in the mud and forced to walk a long ways his whole life. This was just like summer camp to him.

His roommate that summer was a boy from Louisiana. Tad Dumont was his name but everybody called him Doo. Everyone at West Point had nicknames. Luckily John Tanner was already called JT so his just stuck.

Doo was a slow talker and he always had a story to tell. He was good company for JT and they got along perfectly. Doo also played on the football team. He was a tackle and was pretty big compared to JT. JT was tall but slim whereas Doo was tall and huge. He had a tougher time in the physical drills but he kept at it until his time was as good as his classmates.

The cadets learn quickly that no one is a quitter. The decision to quit is not yours alone. It affects the entire company and you soon learn the Army is not about you, it's about the Army as a whole. They support each other and drive the other cadets to try harder until they all make the cut. To JT it was like a football team. You just don't let your teammates down.

West Point cadets enforce their own Honor Code. "A cadet will not lie, cheat, or steal". When a cadet is charged with an honors violation they go before the Honors Committee made up of their peers. The cadet is allowed to bring one cadet adviser with him. The adviser can offer strategy, pass notes and give moral support. A Judge Advocate General or JAG lawyer sits in on the proceedings to make sure the hearing stays within the lines. If a cadet is found guilty, it results in immediate dismissal.

JT always listened and paid attention to the rules as the last thing he wanted was to lose the right to be a cadet. He was a stickler for obeying all the rules and cautioned his roommate to do the same.

JT wrote home often and the rest of the family received a report from Katie or James. James had taken it upon himself to be his brother's keeper. He didn't have a family of his own so he closely watched his brother's life at the academy and offered advice when asked.

Joseph took an interest too but he had just become a new father and he was preoccupied with raising his own family. He spent a lot of time on his farm putting in crops and raising livestock plus he worked full time at a factory in town. On Sundays they went to church and then had dinner at his mothers' and he and James played cards with various family members who dropped in for the afternoon.

Katie was becoming a grandmother quite often. Maria and Grant welcomed a baby girl and Marjorie and her new husband had a set of twin boys. Katie was crocheting every chance she got. New booties and bonnets and sweaters were dangling from every spare hanging post in the house from her bed to the clothes tree to the lamp in the living room.

James complained that the house was beginning to look like a babies department in the local store but he smiled while saying it.

CHAPTER SIXTEEN

LIFE FOLLOWING the war was very good, economically speaking. The factories were growing. When the women left the factories to stay home and raise their families, they were replaced by the men who had returned from the war.

A lot of changes were in the making and new ideas brought new products and the emergence of the television industry. It was the lucky family who owned a television set. Many families would drive into town on a Friday night just to stand outside the furniture store and watch the television that was placed in the store's front window.

Irene was planning a trip to Hawaii to see her new niece. Maria was very excited about her coming all that way, although a bit apprehensive about her traveling by herself. She really wanted Katie to accompany her. She thought the change of pace would be good for her mother but Katie wanted nothing to do with flying on an airplane. Irene ended up flying by herself to California where she was met by her sister Marjorie and Fred so she had the chance to meet her twin nephews too before departing for Hawaii. She was introduced to a couple Navy buddies of Fred while she was there. She had a great time enjoying the sights of San Diego and Coronado. She thought she might move there if things worked out okay when she returned to San Diego on her way home.

"Franklin just might have a fight on his hands" Marjorie told Fred after they had seen Irene off on her flight. "I would love to have my sister close by but I don't want to see Franklin hurt either."

"Honey, there's not a thing we can do about your sister's love life, so quit worrying about it." Fred just wanted to get his family home so he could work on the addition they were putting on the new bungalow they had just purchased on Coronado Island. He was very grateful the war was over. He had found a good paying job in this beautiful city. He loved his boys and his wife and he had to pinch himself every so often to be assured it was for real.

Irene loved Hawaii too and was quite taken with her little niece. Maria and Grant had named their little girl Lani Maureen MacGregor. She looked a lot like Maria but had her father's blue eyes.

Maria took Irene all over the islands and by the time she left Marjorie was sure she would be back. Grant and Maria had a little house not too far from the base at Pearl Harbor. It had been sad to see the battle ship Arizona lying still beneath the sea, with all those sailors entombed inside. It was a sobering experience to see such a tragedy in the beauty of the islands.

Maria talked to her sister about her relationship with Franklin but Irene didn't have a lot to say. She was thinking of the man she had met in San Diego. His name was Scott Hanson and he had swept her right off her feet. She couldn't wait to see him again. Nothing Maria said would dissuade her resolve to call him just as soon as she got back to Marjorie's house.

"These sailor types are just looking for an easy girl, Irene," Maria tried to explain. "I see them all the time over here, whistling at every girl who walks by. They just want a one night stand and that's it."

"Oh Maria, I know what I'm doing," Irene insisted. "Don't worry about me. I think Scott is a great guy. I know he's in love with me and it's my turn for some happiness. You and Irene have wonderful husbands who love you and beautiful children who adore you. That's what I want too! Can't you see that, Maria? Don't you want me to be happy?"

"I want you to be safe. You're my little sister and I care about you very much." Maria took her sister's hands and looked her right in the eye. "If this is true love, after just two days of being together, then it will stand the test of you going back home. Don't rush into anything, honey. That's all I'm saying. Give it some time, until you're sure."

Irene hugged her sister and said she would try to follow her advice. When she left the next day, Maria was very concerned her sister would throw caution to the winds.

Maria was right. When Irene got back to San Diego she met Scott for a date and Marjorie didn't see her sister for four days. By the time she tracked her down, Marjorie and Fred were beside themselves with fear and anger. They found Irene at a motel in Chula Vista in a seedy part of town. A friend of Scott had given them information where Irene could be found. Scott had shipped out that morning and only Irene was in the room when they arrived.

When they opened the door to the motel room their hearts just sunk. All their anger dissipated at once. Irene was lying on the dingy bed, her face a mass of bruises. Her nose was broken and she had a black eye and numerous black and blue marks on her arms and on her neck.

"Oh my God," wailed Maria as she rushed forward and took her sister into her arms. "What on earth happened? Fred, let's get her to the hospital. You help her up and I'll grab her purse."

Fred picked Irene up as gently as he could and carried her outside to the car. Irene hadn't spoken a single word. She moaned a little bit as she was moved from the bed but other than that she was silent all the way to the hospital.

Fred told Marjorie that he would drop them off and he would be back after he made a report to the Navy office in Coronado. With any luck they would see that Scott Hanson was returned to San Diego and face charges of assault and battery.

Marjorie stayed with Irene until all her wounds were taken care of and she was placed in a room. They were keeping her still as she had a concussion along with the broken nose and a fractured jaw. She was not a pretty sight. Marjorie wondered how anyone could do such a terrible and vicious thing to another human being, much less a beautiful girl like her sister. She was so angry she couldn't think straight, but she had to be strong forIrene.

Three days passed before Irene felt well enough to speak. She couldn't talk very well so she wrote everything out on a paper tablet Marjorie had thought to bring to the hospital. She explained that she and Scott had been having a good time but then he began drinking and when she had asked him to stop drinking he had become enraged and began knocking her around.

The military police took a statement and so did the Chula Vista Police Department but they informed Fred that it was unlikely Scott would ever be charged. He was at sea and the Navy tended to keep their men on assignment once the ship left port.

Marjorie didn't want Katie to know of the assault so she and Fred took Irene home with them until she was healed and able to make the trip home. They sent a letter to Franklin telling him Irene had been injured and that she would be returning to Pennsylvania when she had fully recuperated.

Needless to say Franklin left immediately and rushed to her side in San Diego. Irene begged her sister and brother-in-law not to say anything so they honored her wishes and kept still.

Irene and Franklin left for home six weeks after his arrival in San Diego. By that time her wires were removed from her jaw. He never questioned Irene about her injuries but he felt when she was back to her normal self she would tell him. He loved her beyond words and nothing she could say would ever make him feel otherwise.

Irene just prayed that she wasn't pregnant. Maybe it was just the trauma from the beating that caused her to be late that month. Franklin had been so wonderful to her. She wouldn't be able to tell him if it were true. Maria had been so right and she refused to listen. What would her mother and her brothers and sisters say? She would never live it down. She felt so dirty, so guilty and so untouchable. She just wanted to die.

When Franklin dropped her off at her apartment he told her to go to bed and he would check on her in the morning. He had been so gentle and caring with her. She wanted to explain everything to him but she just couldn't. Not yet, not until after she had seen a doctor. She decided she would sleep on it and maybe in the morning it would all be better.

Franklin was knocking on her door before she was even fully dressed. She had slept very little and was worn out. Her eyes were red from crying. Franklin was shocked to see her like this. He made her sit down while he went into the kitchen to make her coffee. When he came back into the living room he gave her the coffee and then took a seat next to her.

"Irene, whatever is troubling you, just tell me. I'm not going to run away from whatever you have to say. I have loved you for years and that will never change, no matter what. Let me help you, please!"

He was so gentle and kind that Irene just began sobbing and became so distraught that Franklin was afraid she was going to physically collapse. He held her in his arms and refused to let her go until she did collapse, but just from exhaustion.

"Oh Franklin," she sniffled into his shoulder. "It was so terrible and I feel so rotten and full of shame. I am so unworthy of your love. You should walk right out of here and never come back."

"Irene, my darling girl, whatever happened we can fix it. Now stop crying and let's talk about it. I promise you, together, we will make it right. Just don't cry anymore. Please baby, don't cry."

Irene told him all about her affair with the sailor and how he had beaten her to within an inch of taking her life. She included her fear of being pregnant with Scott's child. She cried some more and when she stopped crying and looked at Franklin, she could see tears in his eyes too.

Franklin was angry too. Not at Irene, but at the man who could have done such a thing to the woman he loved. He fervently hoped the navy would send him back to the states to pay for this horrible deed.

Irene and Franklin were married the very next weekend in a small Catholic church in French Creek, New York. Katie was delighted her daughter had come to her senses and had agreed to marry Franklin. Katie adored him and thought they were a perfect couple.

Eight months later when little Maggie Sue was born, no one was the wiser. She actually looked just like Franklin. He adored her. He and Irene and their daughter were seen every day, walking to the park and around town. They were a very happy family.

CHAPTER SEVENTEEN

JOHN TANNER was in his last year at West Point. He had made it to the fourth year. He not only was graduating, but he was the First Captain of the United States Military Academy. He commanded over a thousand men. He had the ring. He was a tough, square jawed military man. He was a born leader. The troops under his command followed him without question. They believed in him and his ability to keep them out of harm's way.

John Tanner was headed for Military Intelligence. It's what he wanted to do and what he was best suited to do. He was extremely intelligent and had a sixth sense about him. On Branch Night he was worried he'd get Infantry or Armor. But, he lucked out and got just what he wanted.

Graduation Day was perfect. The sun was shining and everyone was happy and in good spirits. Katie was there with his brothers Joseph and James. Irene and Franklin had driven down and brought his new niece, Maggie Sue.

Of course Senator Quinn and his wife were there. They were singing his praises to anyone who would listen. The Senator explained why Mori wasn't with them. She had just graduated from the private high school she was attending and was in Paris with friends. John Tanner missed seeing his friend. He felt a personal attachment to her as they had been exchanging letters for the past ten years.

Senator Quinn requested he stop in at the Capitol and meet his colleagues before he began his overseas assignment. He extended an invitation to have dinner afterwards with him and his wife and Mori. John Tanner gratefully accepted.

The family departed together. They were driving into New York City for a few days. Katie thought it would be a good time to revisit Ellis Island. She thought it would be a great opportunity to tell her children all about her first hours ashore in America.

John Tanner was so glad they had come to his graduation from West Point. He noticed his mother was getting older. Had she always been this tiny? He thought he saw a few more white hairs on her coifed head. He gave her a long hug and told her he loved her so much. He towered over her and she could feel his strength in the hug. She thought he was a grand specimen of manhood. She looked forward to the day he would find a woman who shared his passion and dreams.

John Tanner's one regret was that his father wasn't there to see him commissioned an officer in the United States Army. His mother had pressed some money into his hand before she left. She explained that when she and JT's dad found out about his acceptance into the academy, they had begun a savings account to be given to him on the day he graduated. She told JT how proud his father had been of his youngest son. That meant more to John Tanner than anything that happened to him on that day. He made a silent vow to his dad that whatever he did in his life it would be done with honor and always in his father's memory.

Now he was a 2nd lieutenant and heading out for his first assignment. First he was headed for Louisiana with his friend Doo. He and his friend had made it through West Point together. Doo was going to Fort Campbell for training. That's where he would receive his training in Airborne. They were going to do some duck hunting and check out the southern girls.

The men were met with jubilant shouts from the household staff assembled on the porch of the Dumont home. What a beautiful place, JT thought as they turned into the drive. Tall pines lined the drive and giant billowing willow trees swayed and bowed in the breeze as the grand, white Georgian mansion came into view.

JT whistled loudly as the car stopped in front of the house. They had driven Doo's convertible down from Baton Rouge. Before JT could climb out of the car, Doo had leaped out and was running forward, only to be crushed in a hug by his father, Tad Dumont the Third.

Seconds later, JT was captured in a hug too and slapped on the back so hard he thought he would lose a lung. The elder Dumont was a huge guy, even bigger than Doo and that was saying a lot. It was certain that both of them came from sturdy stock!

"Welcome home! Go on up and stow your stuff and we'll meet for drinks in the library as soon as you all are ready for one!"

One of the household staff led JT to his room at the top of the circular stairway. The house looked straight out of a Civil War novel, JT thought as he looked around at the massive entryway. Doo had never said his family was wealthy. JT had met his mother once at the academy. She seemed very nice and down to earth. She spoke properly and had a defined southern drawl. Doo said she was a socialite, whatever that was. He knew Mr. Dumont was a businessman. Something in cotton and textiles, Doo had mentioned.

The next three days were a whirlwind of activities. JT met more southern women than he could ever remember. They were always giggling and fanning themselves and he wasn't sure if he liked that or not. Doo liked one girl in particular. Her name was Betsy. She had just graduated from a small private college in the state. They had been lovers since high school. They were expected to get married now that they both had graduated. Betsy certainly behaved like it was a done deal. John Tanner didn't think Doo was quite as thrilled about the idea of getting married before he had even started his career as a soldier.

John Tanner was anxious to begin his training too. Now that the academy was behind him, he looked forward to going to Washington D.C. to begin a new career. That's where the action was. He had heard rumors of a new space program in the works. He could hardly wait to be a part of that!

Today Mr. Dumont, Doo and JT were going quail hunting. JT had seen plenty of guns in his young lifetime, but never the array displayed before him. "Name your firepower gentlemen!" declared Mr. Dumont as he loaded up the truck. "Grab a few boxes of ammunition and let's hit the road." JT was over six feet tall but Mr. Dumont towered over him and outweighed him by about sixty pounds. A bear of a man, he strode about his property like the cock of the walk! A man of great authority, surrounded by his yes men, he dominated the playing field.

John Tanner thought Madeline Dumont was an engaging woman, but she was a bit fearful of her husband. Mrs. Dumont was a pure southern belle. Her world revolved around her children, social activities and her close friends. She knew her place in the household and was mistress of her home but stepped lightly around her spouse.

JT and Madeline had felt a spark when they were first introduced. All they had done was exchange a look or two since that fateful day. Maybe JT had held on to her hand a bit too long a few times in greeting but that was it. Now here he was in her home. He wouldn't want the senior Dumont to suspect anything.

The hunting trip went by without incident. JT participated but his heart wasn't in it. He could tell Doo's wasn't either. He trudged along after his dad, dutifully playing by the rules. He had to bag a few birds or feel unworthy. JT enjoyed the time in the outdoors as it reminded him of back home. He joined in the hunt to please his host. He made a great shot, bringing two birds down with one bullet. That was met with great acclaim from the other hunters.

Mrs. Dumont had planned a dinner party that evening. It was to be held on the verandah. It was a farewell party for her son and JT. The hunting party returned home early so everyone could prepare for the evening's festivities. Tomorrow JT would leave. He was more than ready. New challenges lay ahead and the excitement was building every minute. He was anxious to get started on his new career.

CHAPTER EIGHTEEN

THE MOON was full, the evening was warm, fireflies danced on the lawn. Paper lanterns swung festively over the tables and dance floor on the great verandah. The sweet smell of magnolia blossoms and honeysuckle was carried along with the gentle breeze.

"Just a perfect evening for romance," Doo chortled as he lifted his glass to JT's in a toast before the guests began arriving.

"Thank you for inviting me, Doo. I've had a wonderful time."

"Hey man, the fun's just beginning! I've seen the way Sally Portman has been looking at you! Tonight could be the night, my friend!" He gave his friend a poke in the ribs.

"Yeah, right. I'm not the one expected to get engaged tonight! I bet Betsy is wetting her pants right now, just knowing tonight's the night! Am I right? Do you have the ring?"

Doo looked as if he had been sucker punched. "Don't say that JT! I know my parents are expecting it and so are hers, but damn, I just can't do it." Doo looked so forlorn that JT felt sorry for the remarks he had just made.

"Damn, Doo, I'm sorry man. I was just kidding. Hey, if you're not ready for this, don't do it. Be your own man for a change. You're leaving to begin your career. You don't have to do this. I can tell you're not ready for this kind of commitment to Betsy. Take my advice for once. Go to her house and talk this out before the evening is shot to hell. She'll understand. Maybe she has reservations too."

Doo walked over to the end of the porch and stood with his hands in his pockets, staring out into the woods. JT leaned agaist the porch railing waiting for his friend to respond.

Doo eventually turned and addressed his friend. "You're right. I'm not going to wait for Betsy to get here. I'm going to drive over there and tell her before the party starts. She can accept it and return to the party with me or I'll come back alone. Either way it will be straight between us. Thanks buddy. I owe you one." The men shook hands and slapped each other on the back before Doo descended the steps and got into his car.

"Now where in thunder is that boy going right before the damned party starts?" Mr. Dumont raged as he came out of the house just in time to see the taillights disappear around the curve of the driveway.

"He had an errand to run, Sir," JT replied before turning and walking back into the house. He didn't want to get involved in a conversation about his friend. He had already figured out that Mr. Dumont expected his only son to do his bidding the rest of his life. JT knew Doo was a good soldier. He did a fine job in the field. He had the respect of his peers but something was missing. He was never satisfied with his achievements. Now JT knew what it was Doo was looking for. Approval. His friend needed approval and praise for everything he did. He didn't get it at home from his father.

The guests soon began arriving so JT went out into the yard to greet everyone and offer his services as an escort. Maybe one of the young ladies would meet him and make eye contact instead of giggling like a crazy love-starved schoolgirl.

Doo didn't return until very late. Betsy wasn't with him. Her parents didn't come either. That put a damper on the evening. Mr. Dumont was very agitated and kept looking for his son, but Doo was nowhere to be seen. Mrs. Dumont was trying to be the perfect hostess but her eyes were constantly darting about the room. She desperately wanted to see Doo flirting with all the women and having a good time. She knew her husband's displeasure with his son could affect her as well as him! This was his party and Tad Dumont the Third would never let him forget it!

JT excused himself before the music started and the dancing began. He went to look for his friend. He walked over the entire grounds before he finding him down by one of the sheds, sitting on an old wooden bench. Doo was absentmindedly whittling on a stick he had picked up from the ground. He looked like he had been crying.

JT approached quietly and laid his hand on Doo's shoulder. "What's going on buddy? Did it go badly?"

"Let's just say it didn't go well. She was really okay with it, but then her mother got hysterical. Her father glared at me and told me to get off their property, so I left. I don't know JT, maybe I should never have gone to the academy. Maybe I should have stayed here, gone to a local college and worked with my dad."

"You're a good man, Doo. You love the military. You're going to be a great leader and an ace pilot. Hell, I bet you even make it to astronaut training someday! There's plenty of time for marriage and kids and all of that. Come on, let's go back to the party and see what happens. Everything will be okay, you'll see."

When they walked toward the house, Doo spotted Betsy right away. She had just arrived. She was a bit more subdued than usual, but once he took her arm and said her name they embraced. The party seemed to come alive as the tension evaporated.

JT was full to the hilt with good food and a few drinks. He had danced with quite a few girls. No one had tempted him except for Madeline Dumont. Now there was a high spirited, sexy woman.

JT was always a gentleman but he could have easily lost that title if Madeline had been single and not his best friend's mother. If she had come on to him he wasn't sure he could have restrained his rampant libido. He guessed it was time he left for training. Things were a bit too complicated here.

The party had ended when JT went into the house. Mr. Dumont was in his study making a few phone calls. He came out and immediately went upstairs to his room. Mrs. Dumont had already excused herself and was in her bedroom preparing for bed.

Doo had taken Betsy home. He told JT not to expect him any time soon. JT wasn't tired. He didn't feel like packing. He finally decided to take a walk before retiring for the night. He would just get up early to pack before leaving for the train station.

He walked down by the barns. He stopped to watch a cat who was stalking a mouse in the field. He heard noises in the barn where the horses were stabled so he began walking in that direction. He peered around the corner of the barn and almost fell to his knees in shock and astonishment. There, mounting a huge black stallion, wearing full KKK regalia, was none other than Tad Dumont the Third. He was wearing a brightly colored robe with designs running through it. The horse was also wearing a hood with just its eyes showing. The stallion was stomping its hooves as if impatient to get out of the barn.

Mr. Dumont was yelling something at the stable boy who was trying to hold on to the reins and keep the horse under control. Suddenly the horseman spurred the horse and they charged out of the barn. Their abrupt departure nearly knocked their stunned observer aside, it was so powerful. JT gathered his wits about him and watched until the horse and rider disappeared. He waited until the stable hand breathed a sigh of relief, put some tack away and retired to his quarters. JT quickly saddled a horse and left the barn, following in the direction Mr. Dumont had just taken. He could not believe what he had just seen. He hadn't thought of the Ku Klux Klan in years. You could have knocked him over with a feather in his disbelief. The scene brought back memories he thought were long buried. He rode to the bottom of a small hill and reined in the horse. He quickly dismounted, slapping the hindquarters of his mount and sending him back to the barn. He fell to his belly and cautiously crawled to the top of the hill until he could look down to see what was going on. Several riders were gathered, all robed in white and gathered in a circle around Mr. Dumont. A few of the men were erecting a large wooden cross. It looked like a telephone pole, the beams were that large. A few of the men had come in cars and pickup trucks. JT estimated fifty or more men were assembled in the field below. When the cross was up, everything was quiet. JT knew someone was saying something but the words were garbled.

He didn't know what to do. His mind was trying to sort out his options when two men on horseback rode into the circle dragging a body behind. JT could see it was a black man, dazed and bleeding. He was sobbing and pleading for his life. The two horsemen dismounted and half dragged, half carried their prisoner before the big stallion. The massive animal was still stomping at the earth and making grunts of displeasure. The mounted rider pulled out a whip and began lashing the poor prisoner with it and shouting in a dialect JT couldn't understand.

The situation became even more chaotic as the cross was doused with gasoline and ignited. Suddenly the scene below looked like hell had erupted and all the devils and demons were exposed in a maelstrom of hate and racism.

JT began running down the hill as fast as his legs could carry him. He ran up to the mounted horsemen and grabbed the young Negro boy out of the arms of his captors. "Run, run" he shouted as the now freed young man ran for his life down the road and into the night until his footsteps became silent and the only sound was the rapid beating of JT's heart.

"What the hell is going on here?" JT demanded as soon as his lungs stopped heaving and he found he could speak. He strode around the circle speaking to the assembled group. "You are all cowards and poor excuses for men! Why do you hide yourselves under a hood and garb yourselves like ghosts? I have known men just like you who go about in darkness frightening innocent people who have done no wrong other than trying to be good Americans! You not only make me sick, you disgrace yourselves, your family and all decent citizens!" With that said, JT spat on the ground and walked away. No one made any effort to stop his departure. They were all quiet as he ascended the hill and disappeared over the rise. The meeting abruptly broke up, their intent disrupted. Only their leader, Mr. Dumont remained in place, still sitting astride his mount. Inside he was seething with rage over what had just taken place. He would be keeping his eye on John Tanner Wjotla. No upstart kid like him would destroy what had taken years to build. The Klan was a way of life in the South. He had risen to the top and by god he wasn't going to be struck down by an arrogant youngster!

John Tanner smoldered in anger all the way back to the house. He was trembling by the time he reached his room. He wanted to leave immediately and never return. He forced himself to calm down. It was hours before he relaxed and drifted off into sleep.

The next morning John Tanner rose early to catch the train into Washington, D.C. He said goodbye to the household staff and thanked them for everything they had done for him. Madeline

Dumont was reading the paper in the breakfast room when he stopped in to say goodbye. She liked JT very much and was sorry to see him leave. He had brought a sense of decency into their home and to her it was a breath of fresh air. She could easily have fallen in love with the handsome 2nd lieutenant if he wasn't her son's best friend.

Doo finally staggered out of bed and leaned over the balcony of the stairs to wave a weak goodbye. Dressed only in his shorts, groggy and unshaven, he was indeed a sight to behold. "Hey Yankee," he mumbled through half a yawn, "I expect only the best from you! I'll meet up with you one of these days, wherever we find ourselves stationed a few months from now. Take care of yourself and watch out for those hoity toity women they have in the big city!"

John Tanner bounded up the stairs and hugged his friend. "You be careful flying all those planes, rebel man! Stay up and fly straight! I'll be looking for you!" Both men were damp around the eyes as they gave each other a salute. JT ran back down the stairs and got into the taxi waiting for him in the drive. Right before he closed the door, Tad Dumont the Third grabbed the handle and leaned inside. He was sure in his mind that he had not been recognized by JT the night before, but he wanted to make an effort to defuse the situation.

"I, er, ah, want to thank you for being such a good friend to my son, JT. We all enjoyed having you here and hope you are taking away some good memories." The unspoken words were the loudest. JT could see the sadness in Mr. Dumont's eyes. Whether it was from being found out he was less than perfect, or from knowing he was a failure in this man's eyes, JT could only guess.

"Make it right, sir" was all John Tanner said. Mr. Dumont nodded and firmly closed the door, motioning for the driver to go.

JT would later find out Mr. Dumont never quit the Klan and in later years was brought up on charges following the disappearance of two black men seeking to set up a political rally for a leading black activist.

Second Lieutenant John Tanner Wjotla reported to his unit in Washington D. C. that summer. After a year of intense training he was assigned to a post in Russia. The Cold War provided many opportunities for him to go behind the lines and gather information for the United States. Working undercover he was able to infiltrate communist networks in many countries. He already spoke fluent Polish and he was able to learn Russian very quickly. He loved what he was doing. He was a natural spy. He took chances no one else would try. Several times he was almost caught but each time he escaped. Soon he became known as The Spymaster. He was overseas more than he was home. His family didn't hear from him for months. Their lives went on as usual. New babies were born, families grew and prospered, their world a safe haven due to men like John Tanner.

CHAPTER NINETEEN

MOIRA QUINN had just graduated from the University of Pennsylvania. She had a degree in journalism and was ready to take on the world. Her grandfather helped her secure an internship in Paris with one of the major news services. A few months later she was stationed at the Venice Bureau. She was moving into her first apartment. Her grandparents had just left to fly back to the states. She was on her own for the first time in her adult life.

Mori had hoped John Tanner would come to her graduation. She had invited him but had received no response. The Senator had even tried tracking him down but to no avail. No one knew just where he was. She had always written to him faithfully. When the letters began to be returned, she finally stopped writing. She prayed for him every night. He had always been her hero and would always be in her thoughts. She remembered him as a cadet at West Point, so handsome in his uniform. She had dated, and once she was almost engaged to be married. But, no one could meet her expectations so the relationship withered and died on the vine.

One of the reporters was always asking her out. He was fun and he had a great sense of humor so she dated him a few times. He liked her more than she liked him so it was becoming a bit awkward. Mori wanted someone to knock her off her feet and fall madly in love with her and carry her off into the sunset. She read a lot of romance novels. The hero was always John Tanner.

Perhaps she would never be able to love anyone else if she couldn't get him out of her mind. He was ruining her chances of ever finding true love.

Mori loved Venice. She had been there with her grandparents when she was in high school and always said she would come back someday. She loved the glass shops displaying the beautiful glass sculptures and having lunch in the Piazza. The musicians who played near the cafes were wonderful. She could sit with a cup of tea and a pastry for hours, just listening to the music and daydreaming about life in this beautiful part of the world.

Life was interesting for a young girl in her twenties, living in Venice, Italy in the 1950's. Mori resembled Audrey Hepburn in looks. She was the target of many men looking for a date with the beautiful brunette. She gave few of them the opportunity. She was fun to be with but there was always a hesitation on her part to get serious. The guys she dated always felt like they were being compared with someone on a higher level.

Her job kept her too busy to worry about her love life. Every day was a new challenge and a new story. She decided her true love would show up one day. Until then she would have fun and take each day as it came.

CHAPTER TWENTY

ORI HAD been in Venice six months. She enjoyed living and working in the historic city. She felt like one of the locals as she dashed across the courtyard and entered the building where she worked. Her Italian was getting better and she could converse with the shopkeepers fluently.

Her Bureau Chief was expected in the office this morning. Apparently there was breaking news regarding the Russians military buildup. Mori wondered why countries couldn't just be happy with life as usual instead of always trying to be bigger and better than the other guy. Now it was all about space! Now that was a challenging aspect in today's world!

Moira was doing an article on one of the Basilicas in Venice, preparing for a visit from the Pope. She loved the history of the Golden Basilica. The journey of St. Mark, following his death, was interesting. How many times can a body be displaced for goodness sake? Now the Holy Father was coming to Venice to consecrate a new altar. Maybe she could actually see His Holiness and even have the chance to interview him. Her grandparents would never believe that story!

Mori wondered many times over the next few days where John Tanner was. She tried to trace him down through the news agencies but they didn't have any new information. The rumor was that JT was still in Russia gathering information on the space race. He was working undercover and even those with the highest security clearance didn't know his whereabouts.

Mori wished he would contact her. She missed his letters and words of encouragement. He always seemed interested in her love life. He wanted to know who she was dating and if he was a decent guy to her.

She had work to do so she stopped her mind from wandering, picked up her coat and hurried out the door to greet the day.

CHAPTER TWENTY ONE

A T THAT very moment John Tanner Wjotla was getting off a plane in Pittsburgh, Pennsylvania. He was coming home for the first time in almost four years. He could have knelt and kissed the ground, he was so happy to be back in his home state.

He was exhausted from traveling all over Eastern Europe for four years, gathering information for the American Intelligence Agency. He had heard the rumors and knew someone had tagged him with the name, The Spymaster. It was a thankless job and a very dangerous one.

He traveled freely between Poland and Russia. He knew the language and the terrain. He cherished meeting several aunts, uncles and cousins in Poland. His grandparents had passed on but they left a multitude of relatives behind. They wined and dined him and incessantly asked him questions about his parents and sisters and brothers.

They were very impressed by what Katarzyna and Jan had accomplished in the years since they left their homeland for America. They wished he had brought his mother with him. He couldn't tell them the reason he was there in their country. He said he was on business and left it at that. He promised he would someday bring his mother to Poland to visit them. That seemed to please them immensely.

Poland had been ravaged by war. The people fought for every

scrap of food and clothing. His family had clung to their land and managed to eke out a living from it. John Tanner left them what American money he had as it was worth much more than theirs on the black market.

JT spent years traveling between Poland and Russia, posing as a businessman. He had a few close calls but he managed to talk his way through the interrogations.

The biggest disappointment was not being able to communicate to his family and friends back in the States. They didn't know if he was dead or alive.

The drive to the farm took about three hours. No one knew he was coming so when he pulled into the driveway, he was met with complete silence. He took his suitcase into the house and set it in the living room of the old house. No one was home but he knew James had been there because his coffee cup and breakfast dishes were still in the sink.

JT meandered through the house pausing to touch all the little trinkets he remembered from childhood. He was surprised to discover a new bathroom had been put in. Was that a TV he saw in the living room? Things were really improving in the Wjotla household!

He heard the sound of a tractor starting up so surmised James was in the barn preparing to head for the fields. He quickly ran out of the house and trotted up toward the barn. He was almost at the door when the tractor came roaring out into the bright sunshine.

James took one look at this giant of a man standing in front of the tractor, waving his arms and yelling. He cranked the steering wheel sharply to avoid running over his younger brother. He turned that sputtering machine off and jumped down off his seat so fast JT thought for sure he was going to tumble head over heels down the driveway.

"JT, you devil you! Is it really you?" James was grabbing on to him and shaking him so hard that JT could barely breathe, much less answer his brother.

"James, if you would just let go of me a minute, I would answer all your questions," JT sputtered as he fought to maintain his balance.

"Gawd man, is it really you? I mean, we haven't heard from you in four years or more! Where the hell have you been?" James finally tipped his hat back on his head and took a breath.

"I know, James, I know. I've been all over, just doing my job. For security reasons I couldn't contact you and I'm sorry about that. But, I'm here now and we'll talk about it later. Where's Mama? How's the rest of the family? What's been going on? Is everyone alright?"

The questions were fired so fast James couldn't help but stand there and laugh and shake his head at his brother.

"Hold on a dang minute, JT. Everything in time! You gotta give me a minute to catch up. Your jaw's jabbering so damn fast I lost track of what ya asked five minutes ago! Let's go into the house and get a cup of coffee and then we can sit down and I'll fill you in." James threw his arm around his brother and drew him toward the house. The grin on his face told the world he was in heaven because his little brother was back in the family fold.

James and John Tanner spent the next two hours swapping lies and stories and bringing each other up to date. JT thought his brother's coffee was worse than camel piss and he told him so. James just laughed and slapped his leg. He thought that was hilarious.

A few hours later JT decided it was time to head for town and the Polish Club to see his mom. James promised he would call everyone and try to arrange dinner at the Club that evening for the entire family.

The town of Corry looked the same to JT. He was actually happy to see that because he had pictured it just this way every time his mind drifted back to his home in Pennsylvania. Sure, there were a few new stores, but the layout was exactly the same. They didn't know it but the people walking down the street meant the world to him. He wanted to stop and hug every one of them, whether he knew them or not.

He stopped a few minutes to visit his dad's grave at St. Thomas Cemetery. Tears formed in his eyes as he recalled the day his father died. "I'm home Papa," he whispered. "I saw your family in Poland. They're great people and they are very proud of you, your family and what you accomplished. I am doing well, Papa. I will soon buy a farm here and help to look after Mama. James is doing a good job with the farm. He's a good man."

The drive to the Polish Club only took five minutes. The parking lot was full so he pulled around back. He saw his mother's old Dodge parked in the grass and pulled alongside.

Everyone glanced at him when he walked into the club. The looks told him some were going crazy in their minds trying to place where they knew him from. He took the opportunity to slip into the kitchen. There she was, standing by the stove, cooking up a storm. Her hair was mostly gray now but she was still little and dainty just like he remembered her. She was humming a tune softly as she worked, stirring a pot of who knows what on the stove in front of her. It smelled divine. Onions and peppers and kielbasa he recognized for sure. He could hardly wait to sample some, along with some homemade bread!

Katie sensed someone standing behind her and just as she went to turn around she was gathered up in a ferocious hug that went on forever. "Put me down you big lout or I'll slam this soup ladle alongside your ugly head," she bellored.

JT chuckled and set her down and gave her a big kiss. "Calm down Mama," he laughed, "It's just me, your youngest son, John Tanner Wjotla, home from the Army at last!"

Katie could not believe her eyes. She started to cry and grabbed on to him for all she was worth. She was trying to speak but couldn't stop the flow of tears. Finally they subsided as JT held her and rocked her.

Once again JT had to spend an hour explaining his absence to Katie. She sat him down at a table in the kitchen and gave him something to eat. She wasn't about to leave his side. She looked him over good to make sure he was still the strong young man she had last seen four years before. She thought he looked a little puny so she kept filling up his bowl until he begged her to stop.

"I'm fine, Mama, honest. Everything was delicious, just like I remembered. I am so glad to be home. I promise I will be here for awhile. We will have plenty of time to catch up."

"We will have to call everyone and have them come here for dinner," his mother cried, jumping up to go to the phone.

"No Mama, James is taking care of that," JT replied. "I stopped at the farm first because I had no idea where you would be." He thought he should explain before she thought he took his good ole time to come see his mother! You have to be careful about things like that in a Polish household! Mama is always Number One!

It was a wonderful evening. Joseph and Margaret and their four children came along with Irene and Franklin and their passle of youngsters which totaled five now. Kids were everywhere and JT loved their noisiness and gaiety. His mother delighted in being a grandmother as she scolded one minute and gave hugs and kisses the next. Everyone tried to talk at once. It took three hours before everyone was talked out and left the club carrying tired toddlers and sleepy babies.

JT kissed his mother goodbye and said he would see her the next day. He drove back to the farm, following James in his truck. It felt good to sleep in his old bed even though he had outgrown it a long time ago. As he drifted off to sleep he had a smile on his face. He had come home.

CHAPTER TWENTY TWO

JOHN TANNER wasted no time looking for property to buy. Once he found out the Clough farm was up for sale he went into action. He had wanted that farm his whole life. He longed to see life around the place. He had always pictured cows in the pastures and horses running free in the paddocks. He wanted to dress in old jeans, boots and a hat and dig in the earth, feeling the soil slide through his hands. He wanted to go fishing in the creek behind the barns and hike the woods on the twelve hundred acre property.

Finally the papers were signed and the property went into escrow. Six weeks later JT moved into the house. The Clough farm was officially his at last. He spent the next two months furnishing the house, buying farm equipment and going to livestock auctions. James went with him and helped him select top of the line equipment and livestock. Katie thought he should have some chickens so she took it upon herself to set him up with a few Rhode Island Reds and a flock of white setting hens. She even cleaned the chicken coop and repaired the nesting roosts. Katie still loved her chickens. She told JT that he would thank her some day when he began gathering the eggs!

JT hired a foreman to run the farm. Gustav Weatherup and his family moved into one of the houses originally built to house the farm workers long ago. JT financed the renovation of the house as it was sadly in need of repairs.

Soon the farm was alive with the sounds of tractors plowing

the barren earth. Cows mooed and roosters crowed. JT was in his glory. He went to bed each night totally exhausted and woke up ready to take on another day of fresh air and exercise.

It was a welcome change in his routine. Physically and mentally he was being recharged. The pressure of the last four years had been immense. Now he was feeling relaxed and calm.

Everyone in town and the surrounding areas came by to see what he had done to the place. The men marveled at what he had done in the barns and the fields. The women all wanted to see the house and give their opinions on what more he could do. JT wasn't too interested in ideas for the house but he would listen for hours to the local farmers who offered new ideas for running the farm.

The barns didn't require much repairing. The original builders said the cement barns would stand for a century and they were right. The wooden floors of the cattle stanchions were still solid. The walls and roofs were in perfect condition. Some of the equipment was old and weathered. JT replaced what was necessary.

The old milkhouse needed the floor replaced. JT found several old glass bottles that were still stamped clearly with Spring Valley Farms. He found old refuse from the last operating days of the farm that had been dumped out between the milkhouse and the creek. He found all kinds of stuff in a nearby ditch. The stuff he could use he put in the barns, the rest he threw in a wagon and buried it at the bottom of a side hill in the back of the property.

The kitchen had all new appliances that mostly just sat there. JT was a very basic cook. His mother sent food down the road to him. He often ate at the club or he and James would drive into town and grab a bite at the coffee shop or at one of the bars which lined Main Street and First Avenue.

Irene and Margaret kept telling him he needed a wife. They often invited him to dinner. They would try to fix him up with their single friends. The women adored John Tanner but he wasn't interested. He began to decline their invitations so they finally gave up and just invited him for a meal.

Katie knew he wasn't ready to settle down yet. He had to decide whether he was going back to work for the government or remain a gentleman farmer. She knew that wasn't going to happen. John Tanner had always been a hard man to pin down in one place. He needed action and she knew he would soon be saying his good-byes and heading on down the road. He had accomplished a lot in his young life and there were many more adventures awaiting him before he finally settled down and made this house a home. She would wait patiently for that day.

CHAPTER TWENTY THREE

THE CENTRAL Intelligence Agency had been asking John Tanner to join their ranks for months. He kept putting them off, telling them he was only interested in putting his new home in order. He knew the day would come when he would get antsy and want to take off and save the world again. That was just his way. He was a natural born leader and a true patriot. He couldn't stand the thought of another country trying to pull a fast one. He wanted to be there to help figure out what preventative measures the United States should take.

He finally promised to fly to Washington and talk with the Director. He left the farm in good hands with his new foreman, Gus and his brother James.

The day he arrived at his hotel a message was waiting from Senator Quinn. The message said he would meet him in the Continental Hotel dining room that evening at eight o'clock. JT looked forward to seeing his mentor again. He would finally find out how Mori was doing. It had been a long time since he had heard from her.

His meeting with the CIA Director was scheduled the next morning. JT made phone calls to a few friends and then jumped into the shower to prepare for the evening's meeting with the Senator. He looked very sharp in his gray slacks, light blue shirt, red tie and navy sport coat. Working the farm had done wonders for his physique. He was always a well muscled man, but the sun had given him a bronzed look. He looked like a male model as he walked to the elevator. Women passing him in the hallway turned to give him a second, even a third look of appreciation. JT just gave them a smile and a nod and continued walking.

When he arrived at the entrance to the dining room, the maitre de ushered him to his seat immediately. No keeping the Senator waiting, he mused as he reached the booth where he was sitting. The Senator stood and shook hands. He gave his young friend a hug and slapped him on the back.

"Good to see you John Tanner! You were out of touch a long time! I'm glad to see you looking so well!"

"You look well yourself, Sir," JT replied. " I was going to contact you in the next day or two but you beat me to it! How are Mrs. Quinn and Mori?"

"They are both wonderful. Mori has been in Venice working for Associated Press for about three years now. She was engaged once but it didn't work out. Now she says she is too busy for a relationship! I've always thought she was waiting for you, JT."

JT laughed at that remark. He promised the Senator he would look Mori up if he ever got back to Europe. At that moment their food was served. The two gentlemen enjoyed their meal and talked of other things. Senator Quinn wanted to know everything about the farm. He wanted to visit and see where his granddaughter had been held that fateful time so long ago.

"What are your plans now that you've been discharged from the Army, JT?"

"I really don't know, Sir. I'll be doing something in government service. I am torn between taking care of the farm and returning to Washington. I like the action here. I'm sure I can find a position with one of the agencies."

"JT, I can assure you that would not be a problem at all. Just say the word!" Senator Quinn stated that very firmly.

"Thanks Senator, but I want to do it on my own."

"If you run into any hurdles, just give me a call! You are like a son to me and I want you to be happy!" The Senator's eyes were moist and JT knew he was sincere in his offer.

As they parted ways in the hotel lobby, JT thanked his friend for inviting him to dinner. He also assured the Senator that he would keep in touch with him and would visit him at the Capitol the next time he was in town.

JT went back to his room thinking about the dinner and what their conversation had produced. You were never sure in Washington what the other guy knew about you. Was the Senator fishing or was he just being a good friend to invite JT to dinner? JT had to laugh at himself for being suspicious of his friend and mentor. He concluded he had spent too much time as a secret agent. He suspected everyone of having less than honest thoughts these days.

The next morning the agency car picked him up right on time. The driver never spoke a word but drove straight to CIA Headquarters. He was met by a gentleman who introduced himself and directed him to follow him.

A few minutes later, JT had a badge on his lapel and had passed through several checkpoints within the complex. He was ushered into a large office that had a large picture window overlooking the broad expanse of lawn below.

The Director walked in a few minutes later. After shaking hands, the Director got right to the point. "JT, I want you on-board. I think you would make an excellent training officer and consultant on our team. The United States continues to need top men like you who have done outstanding service to your country.

Tell me you will accept my offer!"

"I appreciate you getting right to the point, Sir. I have considered returning to public service but I'm not sure I want to be in the spy business again."

The Director sat back in his chair and was quiet a few minutes. He leaned forward with his hands together under his chin and looked directly into JT's eyes. "JT, I think you are an honest man. I appreciate you being upfront and forthright with me. I need you. The Agency needs you. The new recruits need you. They are green and lacking in common sense. We can train them to be men of action in the field but we can't teach them to be the leaders they will become down the line. You are a natural. We urgently need your skills in this area. Men follow your orders without question. They trust you and I want my men to be just like you. Will you do it?"

That was quite a tall order. JT appreciated the kind remarks. By the time the Director had finished, he was ready to take on the job this instant. He was confident he could get those greenies ready to play the espionage game!

"I'll consider your offer, Sir, and give you an answer tomorrow. I need a little time to think about my future and consider my options. Give me a quick synopsis of the details and the time I would have to report, and I'll take it from there."

The next hour was spent going over responsibilities and detailed operations. Finally the men came to an agreement.

The Director nodded, stood up and extended his hand. "I look forward to tomorrow then. You'll be doing your country a great service young man. You're very capable and just what America needs in this organization!"

JT didn't sleep much that night. His mind was weighed down with too many questions. What would happen to the farm? Could

Gus and James handle the workload? Would the house be safe from vandals? How would his mother react to him being gone again?

By morning he had his answer. After weighing all the pros and cons he made his decision. He called the Director and accepted his proposal. He thanked him for the consideration and promised to try and fulfill the Director's faith in his abilities.

He was asked to report one month from that day. That would mean he had exactly thirty days to make preparations to relocate to Washington D.C., hand over responsibilities of the farm to James and say goodbye to his mother. JT phoned the Senator but he was out of town for the weekend. JT reminded himself to call him at home. Knowing the rumor mill in the nation's capital, the Senator already knew of his acceptance.

JT flew home that evening. He drove into the driveway of his farm just as the sun was setting. He sat in the car a few minutes, looking over his newly acquired property. "Well, old farm, you sat here alone for a lot of years, untouched. I guess you can get along without me for a few more." With a sigh he walked into the house and headed to his office to begin making plans.

James and Gus promised to take care of the farm and house. James and Joseph would take turns staying in the house at night so no one would think it had been abandoned again.

JT bought a collie shepherd pup from a nearby neighbor. He would grow into a fine watchdog. Just give him a few months and he'd be a great asset to the farm. A few days later he bought another one so each would have a companion. He named them Brutus and Caesar. They immediately set out to run the property as they saw fit. After a few days with them, JT was sure they would frighten away any intruder by their bark if nothing else. They barked at everything, even when the wind blew a leaf off a tree. He was more than ready to leave the farm in their care!

CHAPTER TWENTY FOUR

MARTINA AND Arthur were driving to California for their daughter's wedding. Rose was getting married to a young actor from Hollywood. Martina and Arthur had never met the young man. Once Rose graduated high school she left for New York City to make her way on stage as a singer and dancer. She hadn't done too badly. She landed a job in a chorus line shortly after arriving and between that and waiting tables at a diner, she had paid her own way. She'd been married to a member of the chorus line for a short while. The marriage fell apart when her husband became popular and began to get better offers. That's the way it was in the entertainment world.

Martina and Arthur didn't see her too often. Once in awhile they would travel to New York to see her perform in a show. Usually it seemed she was too busy to pay them much attention but they wanted to assure her they were there supporting her effort to make it on Broadway.

Finally she was offered a part in a Hollywood musical. They heard from her several times a year. Rose had never said she was dating anyone special until she called to say she was engaged.

Martina thought it would be fun to invite her mother along. She had never been out of Pennsylvania. This would be a wonderful opportunity to show her the rest of America. Martina and Arthur had only been as far west as St. Louis so they were excited about going to California.

Katie was beside herself when she read the letter from Martina. First she insisted she couldn't possibly go that distance! She couldn't possibly leave the Club in someone else's hands! Eventually, Margaret and Marjorie talked her into making the trip. James and Joseph also encouraged her to go. Maria promised to come from Hawaii and Irene was positively thrilled she would get to see her mother and sisters.

Katie flew to Washington D.C. She was thrilled with the experience. Imagine flying through the air! John would never have imagined she would be doing that! Arthur was there to pick her up. He had just bought a brand new Buick convertible and was anxious to take it on a cross country trip.

Martina and Arthur lived in Maryland, outside of Baltimore. Their home was quite lovely. It was a single story brick ranch. Katie was quite surprised to see her daughter in these beautiful surroundings. Dr. Matthews had done well with his practice. Katie had only seen Rose a few times growing up. The pictures Martina had mailed to her over the last two years revealed a very lovely young woman.

Martina explained to her mother that she and Arthur weren't exactly pleased that Rose was getting married again at such a young age. Katie just hugged her daughter and told her it would all work out. Arthur was very disappointed in his only child. He grumbled and carried on about the marriage from morning to night. Martina told him they were going to the wedding and that was that so he finally shut up and began packing the car for the trip.

The morning they left was bright and sunny. Everyone was in good spirits as the car left the Baltimore suburbs behind and headed for the golden land called California.

It was great fun seeing the countryside and going through the towns and cities. Katie was having the time of her life. How she wished John was alive and traveling with her. He would have loved this trip.

The motels were small but quaint. Some had breakfast included. Most of the time they stopped at diners or family restaurants which had sprung up near the motels. Katie made sure she checked and rechecked the silverware and dishes. She didn't trust these fast service places. She checked the bedding too at the motels. She was sure there was no way anyone could clean up after everyone who stopped there on a daily basis.

Arthur assured her they would survive this trip. He wasn't sure he would, but it meant a lot to Martina to have her mother along. He took a few deep breaths and kept driving west. He loved Katie and knew she was just being a Polish mother. She was one of the most persnickety women he knew and there was nothing wrong with that!

Route 66 took them all the way from Chicago to California. Arthur promised his wife and Katie that on the return trip they would stop in Las Vegas. It was reputed to be quite the gambling mecca out in the Nevada desert. Katie wasn't sure she wanted to stop where the reputed mobsters hung out but she would keep quiet and let the young people see for themselves. She was just along for the ride and she had to remember to keep her opinions to herself.

Rose met them at their hotel in Pasadena. Arthur had heard of the place from a doctor friend of his who lived there. He told Arthur he was a surgeon to the stars. Arthur didn't know how much of that story was true but he thought Pasadena was a lovely place.

Martina and Katie couldn't get over the palm trees and the bougainvillea that grew everywhere. Katie wanted to see all the gardens and parks that she could while they were there.

Rose drew her mother aside as soon as she could. "Mother," she whined, " please tell me Gramma Wjotla has a decent dress to wear for my wedding. That old rag she's wearing is horrible!"

"Rose Theresa Matthews, that is a terrible thing to say about your grandmother. She has come all this way to see her granddaughter get married and you are worried over her attire! You ought to be ashamed of yourself!" Martina was shaking she was so upset with her daughter.

"I'm sorry, mother, but she will have to buy something suitable before the rehearsal dinner. I will buy her a dress as a gift. How would that be?"

"I guess that would be all right," Martina replied. "Do not embarrass her, Rose, or we will leave before the wedding even takes place!"

"Everyone wears Bermuda shorts and polo shirts here Mother. You and Daddy should wear them too. Put a little fashion into your lives."

"Your father in shorts? Now that would be something," Martina remarked, trying not to laugh. She covered her mouth with her hand to keep from laughing out loud.

The next day Rose took them on a tour of the studio where she worked. They were fascinated by the whole process. Martina loved the action behind the scenes. Like any man, Arthur couldn't take his eyes off the starlets and their limited attire. Katie was just plain overwhelmed by the entire spectacle. Maybe it wasn't such a bad thing that John wasn't here to see this immodesty and decadence, she thought. He might never have wanted to leave. She chuckled to herself just thinking about his reaction!

Rose wanted to take them to Anaheim and show them the new amusement park that had just had its grand opening. It was called Disneyland, after its founder, Walt Disney. She hadn't been there but her fiancé, Zack, had gone on Opening Day. He said it was extraordinary. She couldn't wait to go. Unfortunately she was called to work so the next morning the three brave souls headed to Orange County on their own.

Anaheim was a small town. Orange and lemon trees dotted the landscape. Katie thought that was fascinating. That was nothing compared to the new amusement park. Disneyland was a place you couldn't even imagine in your wildest dreams. To the three of them it was a fantasy, just like the name implied. It was a very warm day, but the excitement made them forget their thirst and discomfort. It was a wonderful place. Katie wished all of her children and grandchildren could see this amazing place.

Martina wanted to come back another day but the wedding was just a few days away. They had many things to do to prepare for that affair. Rose met them for lunch the day of the rehearsal dinner. She waited until the meal was done before presenting her grandmother with a large box.

"Grandmother, I wanted to give you something special for coming all this way for my wedding," she gushed as she handed Katie the huge box.

"My goodness, Rose, what can this possibly be?" Katie set the enormous box on the table and remarked how beautifully wrapped the box was. The dress was a beautiful light blue. Rose had included gloves, shoes and even a hat with feathers that matched the blue of the dress.

"This is simply lovely," Katie said with tears streaming down her cheeks. I've never had a dress so beautiful. Not even my wedding dress was as lovely as this. Thank you so much, dear. I will treasure it always." She arose and hugged her granddaughter tightly.

Everyone at the table was struck with an emotion they never expected. To each of them a dress was a dress but to Katie it was this wonderful gift from the gods. They knew at once that Katie had just received one of the few presents in her life that was a dream come true.

The rehearsal went smoothly. Zack Beaufort seemed like a nice young man. He was very attentive to Rose and seemed anxious to marry her. He was polite and courteous to Martina and Arthur and greeted them warmly. He especially loved Katie. He bowed to her and kissed her hand. She thought he was a doll. She told him she would follow him anywhere. Everyone laughed at that and the evening began and ended on a happy note.

Dressing for the wedding the next morning was truly a treat for Katie. She wished John could see her now. She twirled in front of the mirror, giggling like a schoolgirl before her first dance. Martina did her hair and placed the hat carefully on her head. She could see how happy her mother was on this day and was forever grateful they had included her in this wedding experience.

Following the wedding a reception was held at the Beverly Wilshire Hotel. The ballroom was breathtaking. Katie felt like she was Cinderella at the Ball. The bride and groom were the stars but she was a star in her own right.

Fred and Marjorie were at the church and Maria and Grant arrived just as the music began. They exclaimed over their mother and could hardly take their eyes off her to look at the bride! They had never seen their mother in anything but a housedress. She had a Sunday dress which was nice but nothing like what she was wearing today!

The next day Martina and Arthur, Marjorie and Fred, Maria and Grant and Katie met for breakfast and spent the day relaxing around the pool. It took hours catching up on everyone's family and recent activities. Katie was exhausted by early evening so she retired to her room and let the younger adults go out on the town.

Soon it was time to head back home. It was difficult saying goodbye to everyone. Katie had loved the whole visit. She didn't like saying goodbye to her family. They promised they would all come east soon and have a big family reunion.

Katie said they could all come to the farm. She would put them up in JT's house. They all said they would look forward to that!

CHAPTER TWENTY FIVE

J OHN TANNER was going to the second Inaugural Ball of the President of the United States. He was in shock. Why had he received an invitation, he wondered? He had done a good job at his posted assignment. He had a great job with the government. They paid his salary and gave him benefits. He worked under-cover and kept a low profile. Why had he been chosen to receive such a prestigious invitation?

He had been dating a woman from Washington D.C. She was an attorney on the Hill. Perhaps she was the reason for the invi-tation. The relationship wasn't going anywhere as far as JT was concerned. She was out to get a name for herself and he was just a convenient escort. She was a beautiful woman. She was very intel-ligent too. Sable was built like a top model. Her name led one to believe she was a high priced call girl. There were plenty of them in the Capitol City. She had legs that went on forever. JT smiled just thinking about the night ahead.

He finished dressing and put on his shiny patent leather shoes. He looked damn good in his tuxedo. He hated wearing it but you had to do what protocol dictated for an affair as important as an Inaugural Ball. The Inauguration earlier that day had gone off without a hitch.

The country was in good shape. The economy was good, jobs were plentiful and no one was at war. JT did his best to stay ahead of the game. He spent most of his time stateside now. He was sent overseas only if he needed to extract an agent.

Sable thought he was an attaché with the US Embassy. In a way, he was exactly that. At least it gave him enough free time so he could go back to Pennsylvania and check out his farm periodically. James and Gus were doing a great job. The herd of cattle was growing. They'd had a good wheat and corn crop. In a few weeks, weather permitting, they would begin planting.

His mother had enjoyed her trip to California. She wrote him a long letter describing every event in detail. JT chuckled just imagining his mother being the belle of the ball.

That vision returned him to reality in a hurry. He grabbed his keys and hurried to the garage, hoping traffic would be light going into the city. He was to pick up his ride at the embassy. They would drive over to Georgetown and pick up Sable and then go on to the Ball. He hoped his secretary had remembered to pick up flowers for Sable. Just one more thing to worry about!

Sable stretched and sighed with pleasure. Her bed companion leaned over and gathered her back into his arms.

"No, Jeff," she protested slightly, moving into his arms and kissing him on the side of his neck. "JT will be here any moment and I haven't even showered!"

"Who cares about that spy man darling? Aren't I more fun?" He was nuzzling her neck now all the while moving down the length of her body. She was so gorgeous; he loved making love to her.

Reluctantly, Sable finally crawled out of bed and turned on the shower. It was a cold night and snow was forecast for later that evening. How much nicer it would be to stay home and cuddle by the fire with Jeff. She liked JT and thought he was an incredible lover, but Jeff was special. He made her happy. She was tired of playing the political games and just wanted to settle down. The man in her bed at this very minute could be her ticket to the top if she played her cards right.

JT got out of the limo and made his way to the front door. A light snow had begun falling. That's just great, he thought. Sable would complain about her dress and her hair being ruined. He was thinking about going back to the car and getting an umbrella. He paused just long enough to see the front door opening and his date in the arms of someone else! The embrace seemed to go on forever and was pretty intense. As JT stood there, obscured by a large bush, sweet words of parting were overheard by the couple now entwined half in and half out the doorway.

"Ahem, ah….excuse me for interrupting this lovely moment," JT exclaimed as he walked toward the door." I couldn't help noticing, Sir, that your arms are around my date. Ah, the junior senator from Massachusetts is it? Jeffrey Scott, I recall. What exactly is going on here?" JT stood with his arms crossed, bouncing up and down a bit on his toes as he waited for an explanation. He was more amused than upset over the situation.

"Wjotla, I, er…that is…..we, ah….."

"It's unfortunate you witnessed this, JT" Sable rambled, pushing her babbling lover out of the way. "Jeffrey and I are seeing one another now. I was going to tell you tonight. I'm sorry, JT. This was not a pleasant way for you to find out."

"I have no claims on you, Sable. I've always known you were in and out of many beds in this city. It is for the best. I wish you and the junior senator every wish for happiness. Good night!"

Leaving the couple with their mouths open in shock and disbelief, JT turned and walked back to his car. He gave a little wave before getting in and had to chuckle when they slowly raised their hands and waved back. As they drove away, the couple was still standing in the doorway staring after the limo.

"Do you still want to go to the hotel, Sir?" asked his driver.

"Why, certainly, George. Things are looking up already!" JT was actually looking forward to the evening's festivities. He was a free man and there would certainly be many delectable ladies at the hotel. He bet the junior senator from Massachusetts would not be attending this party tonight! He had expected JT to beat the hell out of him. The little punk! He should have shouted, "Boo", and watched the little shit run for cover!

JT was laughing as he exited the car. He turned his face up to catch a few snowflakes as they fell softly, kissing his eyes and lips. This was probably as close as he was going to get to heaven tonight!

The first person he saw as he entered the ballroom was Senator Quinn. He and Genevieve were chatting with the President's Chief of Staff and his wife. Senator Quinn spotted JT and immediately broke off the conversation and excused himself to greet his friend.

"John Tanner, as I live and breathe! It's a pleasure to see you again. Where on earth have you been? Come and say hello to Genevieve. She will be so delighted to see you. It's been a long time."

"JT let himself be drawn over to Mrs. Quinn. As he walked he acknowledged other acquaintances as he made his way across the floor. He nodded to several people he knew and promised to have a chat with them later.

"Would you look at you, you handsome man," Mrs. Quinn spouted, with an air of excitement. "Mori will be beside herself with joy when she sees you! We were talking about you just the other day"

"Mori is here?" asked JT, looking around the room to see if he could spot her dancing. "It's been a real long time since I've seen her. I don't even know if I will recognize her!"

"She's soon to be engaged, John Tanner," Genevieve announced, watching him closely to see his reaction.

"Engaged? She's still a teenager, isn't she?"

"Oh JT, how silly of you" responded Mrs. Quinn. "Why, she's just celebrated her 26th birthday!"

" Wow! You're kidding! It has been a long time, Genevieve. I am amazed so much time has passed. Who is the lucky man?"

John Tanner almost choked when the Senator proudly announced, "The junior senator from Massachusetts, Jeff Scott! A fine young man, you'd like him JT. The older man lowered his voice and spoke directly to JT. "Mrs. Quinn and I always hoped you and Mori would be a couple someday, but sadly, that hasn't happened."

"How well do you know this guy?" asked JT.

" What do you mean, JT? Jeff's a little fiery sometimes, but his position in the Senate is well accepted and his platform is appealing to both parties. Genevieve and I think he's a fine choice for our Mori."

JT excused himself and walked outside to give this matter some thought. Hadn't he just seen the junior senator from Massachusetts embraced in the arms of his ex girlfriend? He should have punched him in the face and beat the crap out of him! Just then he noticed the two timing jerk exiting the men's room. He walked up to the unsuspecting clout, grabbed him by the arm, none too gently and marched him into an inner room off the hotel's foyer.

"What the hell are you doing, Wjotla? Have you lost your mind?" Scott winced as he rubbed both arms all the while glaring at JT.

"I just have to settle a few matters, Scott. Tell me you're not the man Senator and Mrs. Quinn just described to me as their granddaughter, Mori's, soon to be fiancé?"

The look in JT's eyes told Jeff that he didn't want to answer yes to that question any time soon.

"I have been dating Mori Quinn for some time. What's it to you?" Seeing the rage in JT's face, he wisely backstepped. "I did ask for her hand in marriage, although I could change my mind, under the circumstances." Jeff moved away slightly and lit a cigarette, stopping to exhale the smoke slowly as he puffed. He began to pace the room, glancing back nervously at the big man standing with his feet planted, staring at his adversary with a menacing look on his face.

"How could one human being be such a weasel and live to talk about it?" seethed John Tanner. "Just looking at you trying to weasel your way out of this predicament makes me want to puke. How could Mori Quinn even think you could be the man for her? She has more sense in one finger than you have in your entire brain! Sable Knight is one thing. She's out to make a name for herself in this town. She chose someone equally sleazy as herself to drag herself through the mud with hoping she would come out smelling like a rose in the process!"

Jeff threw his hands up over his face as if John Tanner was going to punch him in the jaw at any second.

"Okay, okay. I admit I was a bit too hasty in judgment, Wjotla. I saw the opportunity with Mori and felt it was a good political move. I pursued her and she liked me well enough. She's a bit of a prude" he whined. "You know, a man has his needs. I needed a dish like Sable to sweeten my bed at night. You know what I'm talking about, Wjotla! Don't tell me you aren't guilty of the same thing, chasing after Sable's skirt with your tongue hanging out!"

"I'm holding it back, Scott, or you'd be a dead man. You're nothing but scum. I want you to break up with Miss Quinn this very night. In fact, forget it! I don't want you to ever see her again, including tonight. Make up whatever excuses your twisted mind can create and leave her a message. If you ever contact her or her grandparents again, I'll kill you on sight. You know I can do that Scott. I could make you disappear forever if I wanted to. Now get out of my sight!" JT was so angry he could have killed the little twit right then and there and never feel a bit of remorse.

"I'm a member of the United States Senate, Mr. holier-than thou big spy man!" spouted Scott, as he headed toward the doorway, turning to keep an eye on JT. "You can break the news to your precious Mori yourself, asshole!"

"That won't be necessary Mr. Scott." Mori Quinn casually strolled into the room, stopping only to shove Jeff out of her way as she determinedly made strides to reach JT. "I heard every word. If you don't get out of my sight this instant, I just might kill you myself!"

Jeff looked at one and then the other and practically ran out the door, hastily making his escape.

What a gorgeous creature, thought JT as this wildly attractive young woman made her way across the room. She stopped a few feet away and stared at him as his eyes filled with the sight of her. She must have stood about 5 ft 8", weighed about 125 pounds. Her hair was a vibrant brown with reddish highlights. Matched with those intense green eyes, JT couldn't take his eyes off her. Her skin was flawless. Only the upturned nose gave him a glimpse of the six year old he had taken home with him all those years ago.

"Cat got your tongue John Tanner?" she asked, tilting her head up to get a closer look at her childhood hero once again.

"God Mori, that was a spectacular entrance! Scott turned white as a ghost when he saw you standing there. I about melted down to my socks. How did you know we were in here?"

"You could hear the squabbling all the way into the ballroom!

It's made for more gossip than the First Lady's dress.!"

"You look fabulous, little girl! You are far too beautiful to be escorted by the likes of Jeffrey Scott. I can't believe you'd fall for a scumbag like him! How did that happen? Never mind, it doesn't matter. Let's get out of here and go get a cup of coffee. We've got some catching up to do."

It didn't take JT and Mori long to find her grandparents to tell them they were leaving the Ball. They ran into each other as they exited the room. Naturally, Senator Quinn and Mrs. Quinn demanded to know what was going on. Mori said she would explain later. After they were assured she was okay and was with John Tanner, the grandparents were satisfied. The rest of this zany evening would be explained later. What was up with kids these days, they wondered as they watched JT and Mori leave the hotel hand in hand.

CHAPTER TWENTY SIX

JT COLLECTED his driver and had him drive to the embassy so he could pick up his own car. The streets were bare. The snow wasn't sticking to the pavement, not yet anyway. The air was quite brisk and cold so he turned the car's heater on right away. He wasn't sure what was going to take place later this evening. It had certainly been a strange one so far. He was looking forward to it, regardless.

Mori was having the time of her life. She loved adventure. Running into John Tanner was an absolute miracle! She had been regretting the evening's activities. Her grandparents were all ape over Jeffrey Scott, thinking he was going to propose to her. Ewww! That wasn't what she had planned. She wasn't ready to get married. She loved her job as a journalist. Paris was her home. She loved it there.

"Where would you like to go?" JT asked her.

"Anywhere it's warm where we can get a good cup of coffee or hot chocolate" Mori replied with a smile. "Right now I would love to be sitting in front of a warm fire in sweats and slippers."

"I can do the fire and the cocoa, but the slippers and sweats would be a bit too big I'm afraid. How about a warm robe and some socks?"

"Now that sounds like a plan, John Tanner. Where do you live?"

"Now that is classified information Miss Quinn. I'll take you there under cover of darkness but you have to promise not to reveal the whereabouts to anyone!"

He looked so serious Mori didn't know whether to believe him or not. She really had no idea what his job was or where he worked. A wink of his eye assured her he was just kidding. This was the old JT. He always kidded her. She felt comfortable with him. He had always been like a big brother to her. When she first saw him tonight threatening that evil little twerp, she thought he was the most handsome man she had ever seen. He was like a hero on the big screen at the theater. Her heart plummeted to the bottom of her stomach as butterflies fluttered in the empty space.

JT didn't know what Mori was thinking. He sensed she was nervous at first but she seemed to be calming down and returning to the little girl he had always loved and wanted to protect.

JT had a small house outside of Washington in the Virginia countryside. Broad Run Farms was the name of the small community. It had a little pond and a park. Many of the houses had pools. Some had barns and horses. Best of all it had warm brick houses with stone fireplaces!

Mori and JT worked together in the large pine kitchen. JT collected the mugs and fixings for the hot chocolate. Mori searched for marshmallows and a tin of cookies he promised her was in the pantry while he made the cocoa.

The fire was roaring and crackling when they brought the tray into the rec room. They grabbed a couple pillows and took up residence on the carpeted floor. The tray was between them as they made themselves comfortable.

Mori was snuggled in his old flannel robe, buttoned all the way to the top. His socks strung out behind her as she walked from the kitchen. She didn't care, she was warm and feeling very happy. JT thought she was just adorable. It just felt right being together in this house. It was a perfect ending to a less than desirable evening.

They talked about everything. He told her about his years at West Point and his friend Doo. He related stories of his travels in Europe. She told him about her college years and the boys she had dated. She regaled him with stories about her years in Europe and what her career meant to her.

Soon she wanted to know all about his family. She asked about his mother and wanted to know what his sisters and brothers were doing. How many children did they have, where they lived and everything about them.

Before they knew it they had both fallen asleep in front of the fire. When JT awoke he was at first unaware of where he was. He had never just fallen asleep like that! The warm spot by the fireplace had just been too relaxing. He glanced over to look at the figure lying next to him. Mori looked so cute asleep on the floor with his robe spread out around her. She was still in her slip from the night before. His socks were peeking out from under a corner of the robe. The ends were hanging a good six inches from her toes. Her hair was tousled and she was snoring softly.

"You're in love with her, you crazy fool" he whispered to himself. He went upstairs and showered, amazed at the change in his heart and mind. He had to focus on his job. He wasn't ready to settle down. It would soon pass, he reminded himself. She was like a little sister to him for gods sake! No, he was sure he would never feel the same way about Mori Quinn again. There wasn't any use fighting it.

When he came downstairs, Mori was awake and in the kitchen making coffee. She smiled and greeted him warmly. "Guess we fell asleep! I'm sorry I overstayed my welcome on our first date!" She laughed and gave him a wink.

"I apologize for not giving you better accommodations as a guest in my home" JT responded. "Here you are making the coffee too. That is really making me feel bad."

"Let me make some eggs and toast too. I love cooking for someone. I took some great cooking classes in Paris. I don't get to show off too often. Please?"

Who could resist that invitation? They enjoyed breakfast in the warm and cozy kitchen. JT insisted on doing the dishes while Mori took over the shower and got dressed for the day. They both thought the new day was a look into their future. It was a mixture of jubilation and apprehension, tempered with comfort and security. They trusted each other completely. That was a true gift only years of friendship could produce. Although they were experiencing the same feelings, they were reluctant to express them openly. The looks between them revealed the truth, but in a very quiet way.

Mori was sad she had to return to Paris right away. Maybe JT would forget about her and things would go back the way they were. She would just have to see that they didn't.

JT was thinking it was a shame she was leaving so soon. He was thinking of many exciting things they could do together. He wanted to show her the farm and take her to visit his mother and his large extended family. But, like him, she had responsibilities. He would just have to make sure she didn't forget him and return to the way things had been this time yesterday.

By the time they were ready to leave for the city, both of them were anxious to get started on a new relationship together.

CHAPTER TWENTY SEVEN

JT SLOWED, preparing to stop at the intersection leaving the subdivision. A motorcade was passing by led by two police motorcycles, then a limo, another black limo and followed by two additional police motorcycle escorts.

"It must be one of the dignitaries heading home from the round of parties last night," remarked JT. He no sooner got the words out of his mouth when a black sedan charged out of a side road ahead and crashed right into the leading motorcyclists, driving them right to the pavement. At the same instant another sedan took out the rear escort vehicles. Another car pulled up to the motorcade. When it reached the first limo it stopped. Three men jumped out of the car and jerked open the passenger door. A woman began screaming as she was dragged from the car.

By this time men were leaping out of the second limo with guns drawn. Bullets were flying everywhere as JT ran from his car to see what the hell was going on.

"Stay in the car!" he yelled at Mori as she attempted to follow him. "Drive back to the first house and call the police! Hurry!"

JT reached the cars just as the woman was being dragged from the vehicle. Not knowing what was going on, JT threw himself at the assailant, knocking him to the ground. He grabbed the woman and dove for cover in the bushes by the side of the road. Suddenly he felt a sharp pain in his back as a bullet slammed into him.

One of the gunmen was yelling at his accomplices, "We've lost our target. Let's get out of here." The next thing JT heard were tires screeching as several cars took off at once down the highway. At last there was silence.

Sirens were heard, way off in the distance. JT started to rise. He was horrified when he discovered he couldn't move at all. He lay still trying to adjust his breathing before he attempted to move again. He knew he was being lifted up but he couldn't feel a thing. He heard mumbled voices that sounded way off in the distance. He gave himself up to the sweet sleep that kept beckoning him, taking him away from this awful nightmare.

Mori arrived back at the scene just as the first state police vehicle arrived. As she looked around for JT she saw two men assisting an elderly woman. They were helping her into one of the limos as gently as they could. Another man was kneeling by a man lying on the ground at the side of the road. The victim was lying prone, not moving, blood seeping from under his jacket.

"Oh, my god! JT….JT….oh please, God, not John…." Sobbing, she ran to his side and began to lift his head.

"Don't try to move him Ma'am," the man kneeling next to her said softly. "Your friend was shot in the back. We don't want to cause him further injury."

Mori knelt on the ground by JT still holding his hand. She continued talking to him until the medical personnel arrived and took over his care.

The scene was chaos for a few more minutes. Stories were exchanged and soon the facts of what had taken place were revealed. The motorcade was carrying the First Lady back to the family home in the country. It was an attempted kidnapping, thwarted by the quick actions of John Tanner Wjotla.. One Secret Service agent had been killed and two were injured. Two police motorcycle escorts had also been gunned down. The First Lady was shaken by the experience, but not hurt. She couldn't say enough about her hero. She knew that without his quick action, who knows what would have happened to her.

The First Lady was quickly whisked away to the hospital where she could be examined by medical personnel, even though she was adamant that she was not hurt. The president met her there. He was visibly upset and didn't waste any time rushing to his wife's side.

Senator and Mrs.Quinn soon joined Mori at the hospital. They didn't understand how Mori was involved in an incident that happened in the Virginia countryside when she lived in downtown Washington D. C. Why was she wearing the same dress she wore last night? Mori assured them she would explain everything once the situation calmed down and they were assured John Tanner was okay. They hugged Mori and told her not to worry, that everything possible was being done to help JT.

The President immediately assigned protection for Mori and JT. Until the investigation was over, two of the key witnesses to the kidnap attempt had to be protected.

Members of the Secret Service who had accompanied the First Lady had revealed that the thwarted kidnappers spoke Russian. Hopefully, the perpetrators would be tracked down and an arrest would be made soon. The more time that passed, the more difficult it would be to find them before they left the country.

CHAPTER TWENTY EIGHT

THE BULLET had lodged next to the spinal cord. John Tanner had no movement from the waist down. Surgery was the only option and that was a risky decision. Leaving the bullet where it was would mean paralysis and any change of position of the projectile could cause further damage. JT made the decision to operate and take his chances.

James drove Katie down to Washington as soon as they heard the news JT had been shot. The entire incident seemed like something out of a fiction novel to the rest of the Wjotla family. They weren't used to that kind of thing happening in their lives. Men with guns, kidnappings and mayhem were not the normal every day events.

No one actually knew what John Tanner Wjotla did for a living. If he had told them he was a CIA operative they wouldn't have known what he was talking about. "That's nice dear," would have been his mother's response. Work hard and be a good citizen was what parents wished for their children in the years following the two world wars. Forget fighting, just give them peace.

Mori refused to return to Paris until after the surgery. She insisted on being by JT's bedside until the very last minute. JT assured her he would be fine and he'd make good on the promise to take her to see his farm.

It was a long day for everyone. Martina and Arthur came to the hospital with Katie and James. Arthur had been in touch with the doctors who were performing the delicate surgery. He had reassured Katie that they were the best specialists in the nation for this type of surgery. Even so, Katie was on pins and needles. She prayed silently while the hours ticked slowly by. Mori sat with her and held on to her hand. Sometimes she squeezed it so tightly Katie winced. Then Katie would pat her hand and tell her it was alright, she understood.

Katie wondered how her son and Mori had reconnected. No one had filled her in on what was going on between them. She could tell it was serious just by the way they looked at each other in the hospital room. You could cut the tension with a knife. More than once Mori was asked to wait outside while the family was briefed by attending personnel. Katie always pulled her close to her and insisted she stay.

After hours of waiting, the surgeon came into the waiting room and addressed the family and Mori.

"I'm Dr. Thomas, the lead surgeon in the operation. JT got through the surgery in good shape. We removed the bullet and we are confident the spinal cord was saved from further injury. It will take a few days to assess the success of the operation but we remain cautiously optimistic."

James stepped forward and grabbed the man's hand in his own in a very firm manner. "I cannot tell you what this means to my family, Dr. Thomas. What you just said were the greatest words we've ever heard. Thank you, thank you." Tears were in everyone's eyes as they hugged each other. Katie led them all in a brief prayer of thanks before they all began to talk at once.

Mori was in a daze. Had she really heard that JT would be okay? When the words sunk in she fairly danced around the room, hugging Katie and Martina and even clutching James and kissing him on the cheek. James was all flustered and sputtered and stammered while they all watched and laughed at his bewilderment. It was a joyful time. Her grandparents were as relieved as everyone else.

Mori remained behind while the others departed to have a bite to eat and take a nap before returning to the hospital later. She took a nap in the waiting room until the nurse tapped her gently on the shoulder and whispered that she could see John Tanner very briefly.

He looked so beautiful to her. He was sleeping peacefully. She noticed how pale his face was against the white of the sheet. He had suffered so much but now the news was good and he would be okay. She gently brushed her fingers through his hair and kissed his brow.

"I'll be here when you awaken, sweet prince. I'll always be here for you."

CHAPTER TWENTY NINE

JOHN TANNER was glad to be home in Pennsylvania. Weeks of therapy had helped him regain full use of his legs. He was careful not to overdo but little by little he was almost back to his former self. James and Gus wouldn't let him do heavy farm work like throwing around bales of hay or hauling milk cans but he loved to be out on one of the tractors. He was all over the farm plowing and raking the soil, preparing for the spring planting.

The fresh air was good for him. Every night he fell into bed and slept soundly all night. He awoke refreshed and ready to do it all over again.

Mori had returned to Paris. She kept in touch every week. She still had a government agent at her disposal. No arrests had been made in the case. She had the feeling JT knew more than he let on but she didn't pressure him to tell her. The less she knew the better. It would all be resolved soon. She didn't spend her nights worrying or looking over her shoulder constantly.

She loved John Tanner. She was sure of that. She had loved him since she was six years old. When she saw him in Washington it was like someone had shocked her with a cattle prod. He took her breath away.

He was as handsome as ever. He was so tall and so strong. His eyes peered into your soul. He knew everything you felt instantly. He was man of superior intelligence who exuded confidence and trust just by his demeanor. JT was a gentle spirit. She knew that from experience. The best way she could describe him was with five words. He would make it right. He always did.

John Tanner knew he loved Mori. He found himself thinking about her at every turn. Everything he did at the farm he pictured her there beside him. He never got the chance to bring her here to his favorite place. He regretted that. Someday she would come. When she did he would beg her to stay.

CHAPTER THIRTY

BORIS PETRINKO and Mikhail Molnarskov were the two men the federal authorities were looking for. They were Russian nationalists, known agents working for the communist regime as hired killers and thugs. JT had identified them on the spot at the attempted kidnapping of the First Lady and the cold murder of America's finest, good men just doing their job.

JT didn't want protection from the government. He refused to have a guy with less experience than himself, underfoot. The President was briefed by the Director of the CIA. He was finally convinced JT could handle himself. The FBI in northwestern Pennsylvania had been alerted to John Tanner's presence. They were warned to keep an eye out for the two Russians.

The dogs were trained to attack any intruders on the property. James and Gus each kept a firearm close at hand. JT had impressed upon them the danger these men posed if they chose to come after him. The house was well fortified. It would take a very determined individual to plan an assault on that piece of property.

May was the prettiest month of the year. The sun was warm. The flowers and trees were beautiful with fresh green leaves and gorgeous blooms. Mori thought April in Paris was spectacular but seeing the blossoms along the Potomac River simply took her breath away.

She was back from France for good. She had sublet her apartment and was headed the very next morning for Pennsylvania. John Tanner didn't know she was back from her post. He didn't even know she was coming to the farm. That was her secret and she intended to follow through with her plan to surprise him. She had even bought a new car for the trip.

For once her grandparents hadn't tried to talk her out of it. They finally realized Mori was old enough to make her own decisions. She was a well known and respected journalist. She had been making her own decisions for a long time. They were very proud of all she had accomplished. They wished her well. Her grandfather gave her directions to the farm from what he remembered from his chats with JT.

Mori thought she could make the trip in a day. She would leave early in the morning and with luck could be at the farm by late afternoon. It would be easier to find her way around the rural roads in daylight. If there was any trouble she had a backup plan to stay in Pittsburgh at the family home and continue the next morning.

Mori was hoping she could slip away from the government agent who was always close by, observing her every move. She didn't mind having the security when she was overseas, but now she was home and it was becoming a bit annoying.

Oh well, she thought when she spied the black sedan tailing along a few cars back. Enjoy observing my boring life if you want to.

Her first stop was at the Breezewood exit off the Pennsylvania turnpike. Gas was the main objective but a snack was welcome too. She didn't want to make too many stops along the way.

Dave Fisher, her security detail, was so busy keeping an eye on Mori he failed to see the white nondescript car that pulled into the restaurant parking lot. Inside the car were two men, one reading a newspaper and the other perusing the area with a pair of binoculars.

Borris Petrinko and Mikhail Molnarskov had been tailing the

duo for three hours. They knew if they stuck with the girl she would eventually lead them to Wjotla. The big shot, John Tanner Wjotla. They sneered every time they heard that name or read it in the newspaper. There'd been plenty of coverage on that attempted kidnapping incident! He'd really messed up their plans. Soon they would not only kill his girlfriend but John Tanner too. First they'd take some time torturing him, making him pay for the pounding they had received flowing the botched kidnapping of the First Lady. Let him see how the spy game worked. They would deal with that interfering bastard on his own turf. It would be worthy payback for the grief he put them through with their superiors. "Get him or you will die!" had been their orders from Moscow.

They'd kill that worthless agent that was following the girl too. They both agreed he was only interested in chasing the skirt. He never even glanced their way. This sucker would be easy pickings.

Dave Fisher had noticed the car sitting in the parking lot. He'd taken down the license plate number and had already called the vehicle in for a registration check. The report had come back clean but he would be keeping an eye on those two when he pulled out.

His job was to keep the girl safe. It was a long drive to Warren County. He would have plenty to do keeping one eye on Mori Quinn and another watching his back. "Let the games begin," he exclaimed as the vehicles entered the turnpike onramp.

Mori was getting close to Pittsburgh. It was late in the afternoon and rain had begun to fall. Maybe the best thing would be to stay overnight at home and proceed the next morning. She wasn't going to push her luck and be stranded somewhere in unfamiliar territory.

She glanced in her rearview mirror and checked to see if her shadow was still following. She spotted the sedan a few cars back. She waited until a large truck was between her and Fisher, then quickly exited to the right hoping he wouldn't notice her missing for a few minutes. By the time he turned around and retraced the miles to the exit she had taken, she would have disappeared.

She paid the toll and continued to the stop sign and turned right. She pulled off onto a wooded lane where she couldn't be seen from the main highway and watched the traffic exit the turnpike. She didn't see the agent's car. She whooped with joy and continued on her way.

The roads leading to her childhood home were very twisting and curvy. The agent could have lost his way many times if he had tried to stay behind her. The hills were steep and treacherous; especially as the rain continued to pour down so hard it was difficult to see anything through the windshield. The wipers were going full bore but were scarcely affecting the pressure of the rain. Luckily, Mori knew the road by heart. Soon she pulled into the familiar drive and made her way to the garage. Getting out of the car was an effort as the wind slammed the rain against her but she fought her way to the garage door and managed to pull it open. She ran back to the car and drove it safely through the opening. She closed the door and exited the garage through the side door, locking it behind her.

She waited on the porch a few minutes watching the drive to see if she had been followed. Finally she unlocked the front door and entered the house.

Dave Fisher had been fooled completely. He was angry with himself for letting the girl give him the slip. The white sedan was still behind him. They had been fooled too. That was a break. He needed to exit and see if they followed. If they were after Mori, he would have to deal with them first.

He pulled off the turnpike at the next exit. The white car exited too. Dave pretended to have a problem with his tires and pulled over after he left the toll booth. He watched as the white car continued down the road toward the main thoroughfare. The men pulled into a service station and sat there deciding their next move.

"This is just great!" snarled Boris. "What happened to the girl? Apparently that dickhead doesn't know either!"

"Calm down, moron! We know where she was headed. We'll continue on and wait for her in Corry. It's not that big a town. We'll just ask for directions to the Wjotla farm." Mikhail started to pull out of the service station just as the agent's black car pulled up behind him and nudged the back of his car.

"What the hell? Oh crap, now we have to deal with this twit! Okay Boris, stay in the car and we'll see what he does. If he comes up to the window I'll throw open the car door and knock the wind out of him. I'll throw him into the back seat, you keep your gun on him and we'll drive until we find a side road, kill him and dump his ass in the woods."

"He's a federal agent, you dumbass. I am sure he is smarter than you think. Let's just get out of here!"

Just as Fisher got out of his car the white sedan peeled out with its tires screeching and the rear end fishtailing as it struggled to gain speed on the wet pavement. The agent jumped in his car and followed, keeping a close eye on the direction they were taking. He wasn't familiar with the local roads but he was sure they didn't know where they were either. It should be an interesting night.

The two suspects were tired and spent. They just wanted a place to lay their heads for a few hours sleep. The agent had kept a tight distance between the cars. He must be tiring too but he was keeping up with them, just daring them to stop.

They would need gas soon and something to eat. Fisher was counting on that to slow them down. He would love to end this pursuit and bed down for the night.

Suddenly the car he was pursuing took a quick right and sped up a hill. Fisher followed slowing down to avoid a trap. The car turned left at the top of the hill into a drive that was more of a dirt country lane. It dead ended at a shack that was barely standing intact at the edge of the woods. Probably an old hunting camp, Fisher figured. Now what were they going to do? They were trapped. He saw them get out of the car and walk slowly toward his car with their arms partially raised over their heads.

"Stop where you are and get down on the ground," he ordered. "Spread your legs and keep your hands over your head where I can see them."

"We haven't done anything," Boris whined. He was the bigger of the two men. He had to weigh about three hundred pounds and was only about five feet ten inches tall. His arms were muscular. Fisher knew he didn't want to get caught between those two arms that looked like whole hams with biceps.

Mikhail was taller, maybe six two, about two hundred and fifty pounds. They were both dressed in rough cotton work pants with flannel shirts. Their boots were meant for shit kicking, hard soled and meant for action.

'If you aren't guilty of anything, then why are you running? Why are you following me? Your ID is fake and the car's registration doesn't match the names you just gave me. What do you have to say about that?"

Mikhail noticed the agent was standing a few feet away from them. If he could only get his knife out of his boot, he would at least have an advantage. If Boris didn't stop whining, he would be the first to feel the knife go deep into his ribs! Why did he always get stuck with the crybabies?

Fisher was wondering what to do with these characters. They were armed and dangerous and he couldn't transfer them alone. One false move and they would be on him like flies on manure. He should just shoot them and leave them where they lay. He could send the sheriff out to get them when he got back to town.

At that moment a huge buck jumped out of the woods and startled the men half to death. Boris and Mikhail took the opportunity to jump up and tackle Fisher. Fisher's gun went off but the bullet found its target in a tree across the yard.

Mikhail found his knife and plunged it into Fisher's neck and the agent fell dead to the ground.

The two men were breathing hard as they dragged the agent to the woods and threw him into the brush.

"That was convenient," Mikhail acknowledged, wiping his brow with the tail end of his shirt. "Let's get out of here and find a room and some food. We can drive on tomorrow. Nobody will find his body until hunting season."

Boris nodded his head and followed his pal to the car. "Maybe we should leave this one and take his" he said as he gestured toward the agent's black sedan.

"You are such an idiot, nimrod" the younger man replied, looking disgustedly at his partner. "That's an official government vehicle. We would be sitting ducks riding around in that! Now get in the car and shut the hell up!"

Mikhail just shook his head as he turned around and headed back to the main road. One down and two to go. He was ready to complete this mission and get back to Russia. He decided he would rather serve out his days at a desk than put up with this dumb shit partner they gave him. He grumbled all the way to the motel.

CHAPTER THIRTY ONE

ORI DROVE into the farm just as the sun was clearing the clouds. It had been a foggy drive most of the way. She was amazed at how beautiful the house was. It stood so majestically under the tall maple trees that spread over the rooftop like an umbrella, their green leaves forming a blanket of nature's creation.

She was admiring the lovely porch and entry door when two massive beasts came tearing up the drive from the barns, barking and carrying on like a couple of banshees. James came running after them yelling at them to stop.

Mori wasn't afraid of them. She stood firm and when they approached she greeted them by name and spoke gently to each one like they were old friends.

"My goodness, you silly boys. Just look at you guys! You must be Caesar and you are Brutus," she said gleefully as she knelt to hug each one. Caesar gave her a big lick and Brutus laid his massive head on his paws and looked at her so adoringly she had to kiss the top of his head.

"I'm sorry, Mori," James exclaimed as he came to a halt in front of her. These dogs are not friendly to strangers. I tried to tell you to stay in your car but I was too late." James was trying to catch his breath. "They must have taken an instant liking to you."

"I have that effect on men sometimes," Mori said with a chuckle. "Sometimes men just fall to the ground when they see me coming."

James laughed and pointed off in the distance. "John Tanner is out in the orchard trimming the apple trees this morning. Why don't you head that way and I'll take these rascals with me."

"Oh, please James, let them come with me. They won't be any trouble."

"Okay little girl, if you say so. JT will be happy to see you. He's been going around here with his face hanging to the ground like a dadburn bloodhound for too long. Seeing you oughta perk him up."

"I love the farm James. It's beautiful, just like John said it was. I don't remember anything about it. It is always dark in my memories."

"Don't be worrying about none of that stuff Mori. We'll take good care of you. Now get on out there and have fun."

The two dogs ran on ahead, happy to be running loose in the fields. They'd stop and race back to Mori for a pat and then take off running again. Mori was glad she had worn jeans and sneakers. The footing was stony and uneven. She loved the walk. She could see the orchard straight ahead. The trees all had blossoms on them. The air was full of the sweet perfume the blossoms released every spring.

John Tanner heard the dogs before he saw them racing toward him. He wondered what the heck they were doing out here and was getting down from the ladder when he saw a young woman descending the hill. He put his hand up to his face to shield the sun so he could see who it was. He thought maybe it was his sister-in-law, Margaret, but she didn't have any tag along kiddos with her like she usually did.

Mori waved when she saw him looking her way. As she drew closer she saw him remove his hat and start toward her. He had the biggest grin on his face when he recognized her.

JT didn't even wait to say hello. He grabbed her up in a bear hug and swung her around and around before setting her on the ground. The dogs thought this was great fun. They began to bark and wag their tails, trying to get some attention too.

"What are you doing here, young lady? How on earth did you ever find this place? When did you get back from Paris?"

The questions were coming so fast Mori had to throw her head back and laugh. "Slow down JT. I'll answer all your questions one at a time."

"Let's go up to the house and I'll make us some coffee or tea. I want to hear all about how you got here and how long you are staying. God, Mori, you are a sight for sore eyes!"

"How are you feeling, John? You look terrific!" He did look in perfect health. Even in his worn jeans, old denim shirt and aged sneakers, the sight of him made her heart leap.

"I'm doing fine. My back is healed and I haven't had any problems at all. Just a twinge on a cold damp morning is all I can complain about."

He grabbed her hand and led the way across the meadow toward the house. Their conversation was about her trip up from Washington. JT laughed when she told how she ditched her protection agent. He was sure the agent was back on track by this time. He looked across the field to the road but everything was quiet.

The dogs raced each other to the house. They paused to take a drink from their bucket near the back door. Brutus and Caesar had enough exercise for one morning. They collapsed in a heap under a nearby tree panting happily.

JT took Mori on a tour of the house while the water brewed for their beverage. Mori thought it was beautiful. JT had restored the original mouldings and some of the beautiful carpeting. The original dining room furniture was intact and beautifully finished with a lemon polish.

Mori loved the nursery. It still looked like a page from a children's book in the Victorian era. How delightful it would be for a houseful of youngsters. She could almost hear the laughter as she descended the stairs.

John Tanner took special pride in his room. The master suite was huge. The bed was massive. He said it was the original bed of Levi Clough. He had custom ordered the mattress and box spring. The closet was as big as one of the bedrooms. The matching dresser and chest of drawers each had seven drawers. JT said some of them had never been filled.

The kitchen was cozy and warm even though it was very large. It had a fireplace on one end. The stove took up one wall. Whoever did the cooking must be able to do everything in one attempt, Mori thought as she opened one of the ovens.

"Actually, most of the cooking was done in the summer house, adjacent to the house, in the back." JT opened the screen door and showed her the door leading into another complete kitchen. "The intention was to keep the heat out of the house in the summer. I'm sure you've seen similar setups in some of the plantation houses in the south."

Just as the couple was ready to sit and relax over a cup of tea, the phone rang. JT answered it with a smile in his voice but that smile immediately turned to concern. He hung up before sitting back down and directing his attention to Mori.

"That was Dave Fisher's superior. He said Fisher's car was found this morning in western Pennsylvania on a rural road outside of Pittsburgh. There wasn't any sign of the agent but they're searching the area and should know something soon."

"I feel terrible, John. Something has happened to him and I am responsible."

" No, you're not at fault here. Dave Fisher knew what he was doing. Did you observe anyone else following you or see anything out of the ordinary?"

"I really didn't notice anyone but Dave. Wait, on second thought, I did see him speaking to two men in a white car at the restaurant before we got on the turnpike. Do you suppose they had anything to do with Dave's disappearance?"

"I don't know but we should report it anyway."

While JT called Washington, Mori cleaned the kitchen and put the few dishes away in the cupboard. She was worried about Dave Fisher. He was annoying, always following her around, in Paris and now at home. He certainly didn't deserve anything bad to happen to him. He was always pleasant and courteous to her.

CHAPTER THIRTY TWO

ETRINSKI AND Molnarskov were making their way across fields covered in sticker-like plants that attacked them at every turn. "Damn, what are these things?" Boris whined plucking at his shirt sleeve, trying to pull it down. He began to scratch his arm profusely.

"It's just a nettles plant. They are a nuisance but part of the landscape in this area. Their tiny barbs carry a poison that has unpleasant side effects, like itching, but you will survive. I almost think that may be a pity."

"What do you mean by that remark?" Boris whined running to catch up with Mikhail.

"It means you have done nothing but whine for the last two days. I don't like this job any more than you do, but we botched the other one. Now we have to save our asses by eliminating the witnesses. Just shut up and let's get it over with!"

The sun was just coming over the horizon as the two men approached the horse barn.

"Wow, these barns are huge!" exclaimed Boris. "We can't burn them down, the concrete in them must be three foot thick!"

"There are other ways to handle the two of them, Boris. Just a quick shot to the head would be my way. It's quick, less messy and we can be on our way back in less than five minutes."

At that moment, Gus was walking up to the cattle barn. The two dogs were racing toward him from the direction of the house.

Suddenly they turned from Gus and began running toward the horse barn, barking and growling, their hackles rising on their back.

"Quick, get into the barn and close the door!" Mikhail said under his breath as he opened the door on the side of the building. Both men ducked into the opening and slammed the door just as the dogs charged right at them.

"Caesar, Brutus, what the hell are you dogs after now? Gus came panting up behind the barn. The dogs were still barking out of control and scratching at the door. "If that's a squirrel or fox I'm going to have both your hides hanging on the side of my house before nightfall!"

Gus had barely walked into the barn when he was hit from behind and fell to the ground unmoving. Brutus and Caesar charged through the door behind them and met the same fate.

Boris put the shovel down and walked around his victims. "Those are big bruisers, Mik. I wouldn't want them to have a piece of my leg!"

"Get over here Boris! We've got to be ready for them when they come. They must have heard all the commotion by this time. Get ready with your gun and follow my lead. Don't blow it this time!"

John Tanner and Mori were running up to the barn to see what all the commotion was about. The dogs always met Gus in the morning on his way to take care of the cows. They usually didn't carry on like they did today.

JT didn't say anything to Mori but he was more than a bit disturbed by the way Caesar and Brutus were howling and barking. That wasn't normal behavior over a squirrel or chipmunk that crossed their path.

Mori was calling the dogs. When they didn't respond, JT was

really concerned.

"Mori, go back to the house and call the police. Just tell them it's JT at the old Clough farm and they'll take it from there."

"Shouldn't I come with you?" Mori hollered as she began to turn back toward the house.

"No, please, just do as I say, and hurry!" JT watched as Mori raced down the drive toward the house. James was just turning in to the drive when he saw Mori race into the house. Looking toward the barns he saw his brother motion to him to come up the hill but to go to the side of the milk house.

JT walked over to where James was waiting. 'What the hell," James began when JT put his hand over his brother's mouth and cautioned him to be quiet.

"Hush James, I think the two guys who after Mori and me are holed up in the horse barn."

"What?" was the half-sputtered response from James. "Here, at this moment? What makes you think so?" His eyes darted from the barn then back to the house and then back to JT.

"The dogs were going crazy a minute ago, now they're silent. Gus was with them and now I can't get him to respond either. Don't you think that's just a bit strange?"

"What should we do? I've got my hunting rifle in the truck and a skinning knife in the glove compartment."

"Go get them and walk behind the barn and wait for my signal."

"Where will you be, JT? Don't go doing anything stupid. We could just wait for the police you know!"

"I'll be making my way up to the roof. They're not farmers, James, they're hired assassins. This is a game to them. Tell Mori to stay at the house until the police get here. On second thought, tell her to take your truck and get the hell out of here!"

"Where shall I tell her to go? She doesn't know her way around here!"

"Hell James, what difference does that make? I just want her out of here! Now get going before she comes out of the house!"

Taking one last glance at his brother and one at the house, JT scurried around the milk house and ran behind the cattle barn. A jump down to the ditch behind the barn and a crouching dash through the weeds and high brush led him to the side of the horse barn. He looked up to the window on the second story. The tractor was sitting behind the barn. He climbed on top of the seat and looked around for anything that resembled a rope. He couldn't find a rope and his heart sunk. But, wait, wasn't that a hose over by the corral? Why wasn't there a damn rope by the corral? This was a goddamn horse barn!

JT grabbed the hose and threw the one end over the hay hook which protruded from the second story of the barn in front of the door through which the bales of hay were unloaded. He grabbed both ends of the hose and hoisted himself up to the overhanging roof. It was a short step up to the window ledge and within seconds he was inside the barn.

He could hear garbled voices echoing through the huge cavernous structure. Slowly he inched his way forward, careful not to disturb any loose hay or dust that would give away his presence.

JT was filled with scathing hate at the sight of Boris and Mikhail. A glance to his left told the story of what had happened to Gus and his two dogs. They lay lifeless on the ground. JT held himself back from crying out in rage.

The two gunmen were standing by the front of the barn trying to peek through the huge barn doors to see if he was coming up from the house.

JT bided his time until he knew James would be in position as back up. He had the fire power. JT had nothing but his bare hands and army training with a little common sense thrown in.

Above his head he saw the bucket on the conveyor belt used to haul the manure away from the cow stanchions in the winter months when the horses and cattle were kept inside.

He just had to get the men closer to the stanchions. He looked around the area and spotted a lantern up on a shelf. Surely there would be matches nearby. He felt along the shelf until he felt the little wooden box. He breathed a sigh of relief when he saw there were still matches inside.

Leaning over the loft he saw there was hay and bits of straw in the first stanchion. He took a leaf of hay from the bale and set it afire and tossed it down into the stanchion. The two men jumped at the noise and glanced back to see the fire burning. Thinking only of themselves they ran over to try and extinguish the blaze. At that moment, JT released the bucket and sent it on its way down the cable.

The blow from the iron bucket sent the men to their knees. Boris was knocked unconscious but Mikhail staggered to his feet and began shooting. Just then James came hurtling through the back door with his rifle at the ready. The gunman pulled back the front door and ran like hell to get away.

Unfortunately, instead of driving away from the farm, Mori drove toward the barn. She was just attempting to get out of the truck when Mikhail grabbed her and held her hostage with his gun at her head.

"I've got the girl, Wjotla. If you don't show your face in thirty seconds, she's dead."

JT told James to skirt around to the other barn and come up behind the truck. He tried to buy some time talking to Mikhail to give James time to get into position.

"I'm making my way down, Mikhail. You'd better not harm a hair on that girl's head. I'll kill you with my bare hands if you harm her in any way!"

The KGB agent laughed maliciously. "You're not so tough, Wjotla. The Great Spymaster himself! Funny, you don't look so brave standing here unarmed with straw hanging from your clothes."

JT was standing in front of him now, arms at his side, totally defenseless.

"Look at you, asshole, Mr. Dapper Don himself, cow shit hanging from your hair and clothes. That dung on your head might just get inside that bad cut and give you a nasty infection. Now that would be a bad way to die."

Mikhail seemed taken back by that statement. He even wavered a bit trying to brush the manure away from the bleeding cut.

"Just give me the girl and get it over with, Mikhail. You've got the truck. Just get in and drive away, no harm will come to anybody. It will be an agent's truce. What do you say?"

"I am sorry my friend. It has to be this way. I must kill you both or I will be a marked man."

"You're right Mikhail. Just let me hold her and do what you have to do." JT pulled Mori close to him and whispered in her ear not to worry, he had it covered. She was shaking so hard he thought she'd slide right out of his arms but he held her even tighter.

Mikhail raised his gun and in that instant James's skinning knife penetrated his back and he slid to the ground, the gun falling harmlessly next to him.

"Whew, thanks brother. You had me worried there for a minute."

James was kneeling by Mikhail checking his vital signs. "He'll live I think, but he won't be good for much."

"Even if he was rock solid healthy, he'll be dead before his trial ever begins. The Russian network will make sure of that," JT replied. "It's all part of the game."

Mori was crying in relief and refused JT's outstretched arms. She walked right by him and grabbed on to James.

James seized the opportunity to tell her it was alright, he'd take care of her. He suggested they go check on Gus and the dogs so she sniffled into his hanky and together they walked back into the barn.

JT scratched his head in bewilderment and walked down the driveway to greet the sheriff's vehicle that had just arrived.

Boris was dead. Mikhail was barely alive but he would live to stand trial for the attempted kidnapping of the nation's First Lady and the murder of three law enforcement personnel. Later that fall, the remains of David Fisher was discovered by deer hunters.

Gus had a concussion but a few days hospital stay and he was ready to get back on the tractor. The dogs were on house recuperation. They were spoiled terribly by Mori. JT said he didn't think they would ever be good for watch dogs again. He told Mori she might as well put bonnets on them as they were now her pets. Brutus and Caesar were highly offended by that remark and were soon seen back on patrol.

CHAPTER THIRTY THREE

THE NEXT few days were taken up with the attention of the media, the police and the local curiosity seekers invading the property. JT let James and Joseph deal with most of it. He and Mori told their stories to the proper authorities and refused all interviews. In a few days the news died down and everyone went away.

Mori awoke one morning and decided it was such a beautiful warm day that she and JT would take a walk. Just get away and take a picnic lunch. That was the plan. When JT walked into the kitchen she was dressed in shorts and a halter top. She was humming to herself while making sandwiches and cutting up fruit. The smell of fresh baked cookies filled the kitchen with a wonderful aroma.

"What's going on?" he asked as he leaned over and gave her a kiss on the cheek. "It looks like someone is going on a picnic."

"That's what it is! A walk in the woods and a picnic! I thought we could follow the trail that we took that day you rescued me from the KKK. I remember how frightened I was as we walked through those big dark woods. Can we do it again, JT?"

"Sure we can. I don't know what it is, but I seem to have to keep rescuing you from this place. If a walk in the woods would help chase away any lurking demons, I am at your service my lady."

The sun was hot by the time JT and Mori cleared the boundary of the farm and entered the woods. Mori was glad she had worn shorts and a halter top. It was one of those humid days that just melted the socks right off your feet.

JT wasn't into shorts. He was in his normal jeans and a tee shirt. He kept brushing his hair back from his forehead. She could see he was sweating but he would never complain. If Mori wanted to take a hike on the hottest day of the year, he would gladly sweat ten pounds off to oblige her. He wanted to take their relationship further but he was being the perfect gentleman. A few stolen kisses were all that she had allowed. He couldn't live forever on that!

Mori had wondered when JT would make a move toward her. For a man he was mighty slow in the romance department. She was hoping this time by themselves would push things along. This weather certainly wasn't helping the situation. The woods were cool and damp from the morning fog but the open areas where the sun hit were like walking through an oven with air so heavy breathing was difficult.

JT took her hand as they walked along, helping her over branches that had fallen and were covered with slippery moss.

Suddenly Mori let out a little cry and ran forward, literally falling into a creek. She was laughing as she came splashing to the surface, throwing the spray all over JT.

"Oh, JT, this is marvelous! You didn't tell me about this wonderful place! Come on in and join me! It's so refreshing!"

" I, uh, just have jeans on and they're a bit heavy under water."

"Just take them off, silly! I promise not to look. Come on! It feels wonderful. Don't be a party pooper!"

JT wasn't going to put up with that. He stepped out of his jeans and dove right into the creek. He came up gasping with the shock of the cold water. It was still spring and the heat of the sun hadn't penetrated the deep waters.

He swam over to Mori and dove under her and came up with her in his arms. When they reached the surface he threw her away from him and watched as she fell sputtering into the swirling waters.

JT didn't see her surface and was starting to panic when he was grabbed from behind and pushed under the water. When he surfaced he saw Mori standing a few feet away laughing. He loved the way her face scrunched up when she laughed. Her mouth was open and he could hardly keep from covering those red lips with his own. Her nipples were standing at attention from the cold water. As he looked lower he could see the outline of her panties under her shorts and he gasped from the power of his love for her at this very moment. Maybe it was lust but he didn't care. He knew he had loved this woman from the time she was six years old and frightened to death.

The sound of a waterfall drowned out their conversation. They had moved quite a ways down stream in their water play. Thunder was pounding the earth around them as a sudden thunder shower followed the breeze that had just come out of nowhere. Some force neither of them could control moved them under the waterfall and as the powerful down thrust of water cascaded over their bodies they came together in an embrace that neither of them could have prevented or would have wanted to.

They couldn't get enough of each other. JT stared into her eyes as he slowly undressed her. He tossed her clothes on a nearby tree branch. He then slid his undershorts and tee shirt off and tossed them he knew not where.

His hands were all over her body as she touched him where he had longed to be touched for so long.

Her legs encircled his back as he plunged into her and made her his for the first time.

The storm ended as quickly as it came. The waters of the Brokenstraw were churning as were the sexual urgings of Mori and John Tanner. They were exhausted as they exited the creek and wrapped themselves in the blanket they carried for their picnic. The mossy ground made a soft bed for them to lie on. The afternoon was spent discovering each other and making love with the sweet music of the forest enveloping them. The whispering of the leaves as they fluttered in the breeze and the gentle flowing of the water created their own Garden of Eden. They had found each other at last.

EPILOGUE

JOHN TANNER Wjotla and Mori Emily Quinn were married in the Chapel at West Point the following October. They honeymooned in Paris and set up housekeeping at the old Clough Farm in Spring Creek, Pennsylvania.

Nine months later twins were born at the local hospital. A little girl, Katharine Quinn and a little boy, James Pietr.

John Tanner Wjotla later became the Governor of Pennsylvania and was planning a run for the White House.

Katarzyna Magdalena Wjotla loved being a grandmother for the sixteenth time. She spoke to Jan Pietr Wjotla often, telling him stories about how their children were doing. "Imagine Jan, our son, the President of the United States. Remember that night in the barn, Jan? That was the beginning. I loved you so much. I still do"

THE END

ISBN 142514516-7